A STAR WARS STORY

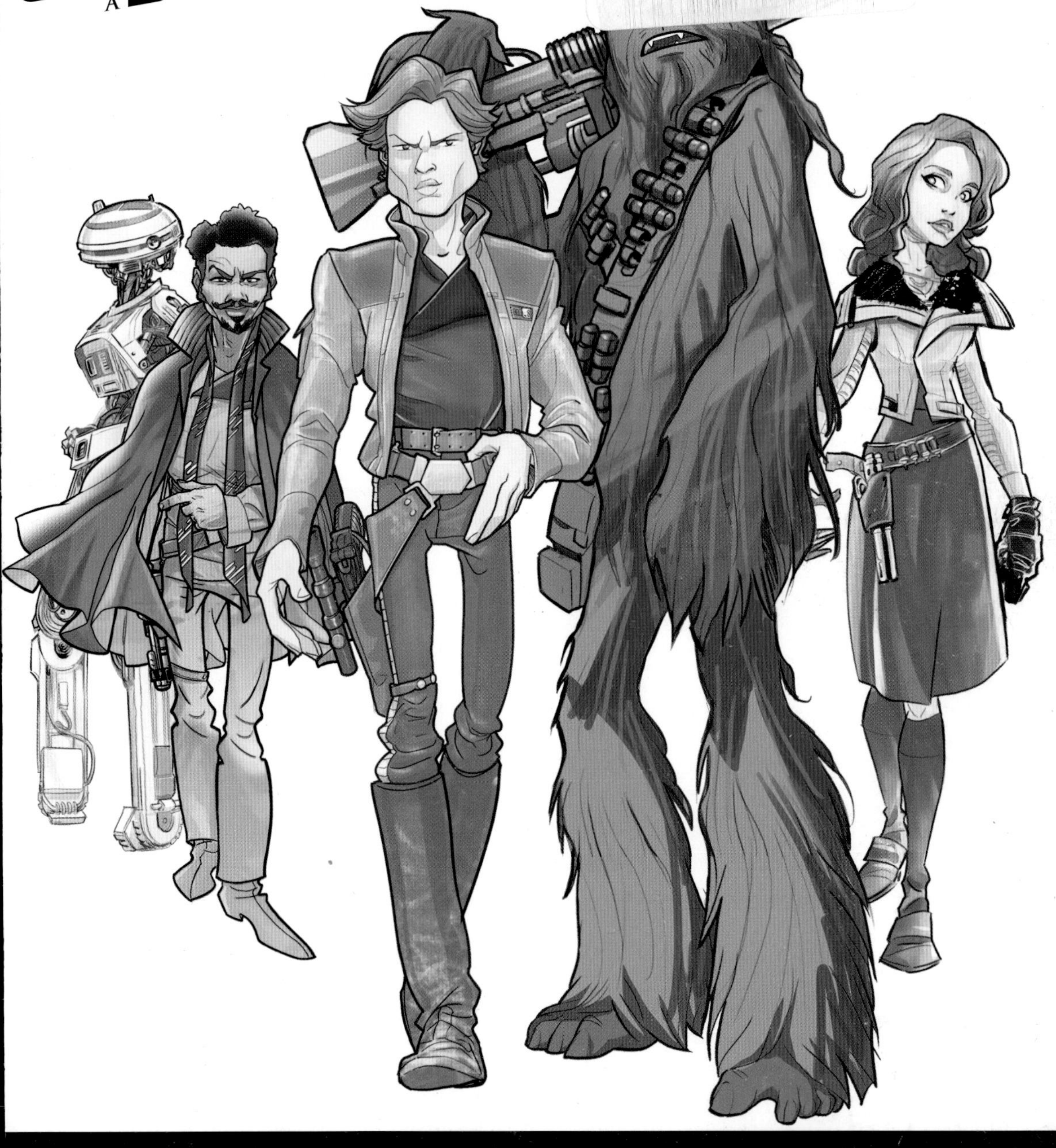

A LONG TIME AGO, IN A GALAXY FAR, FAR AWAY....

Meet the CHARACTERS

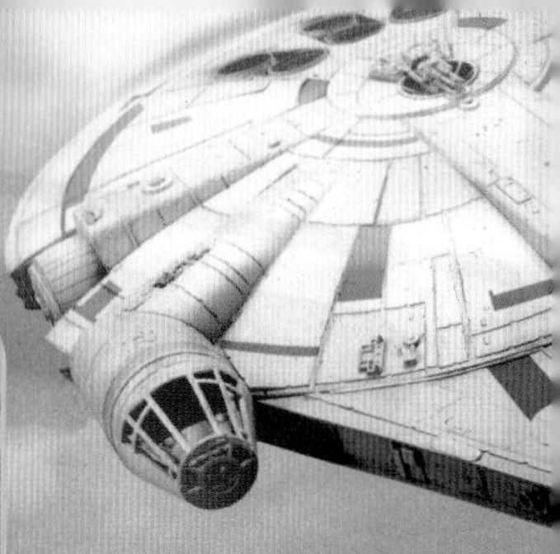

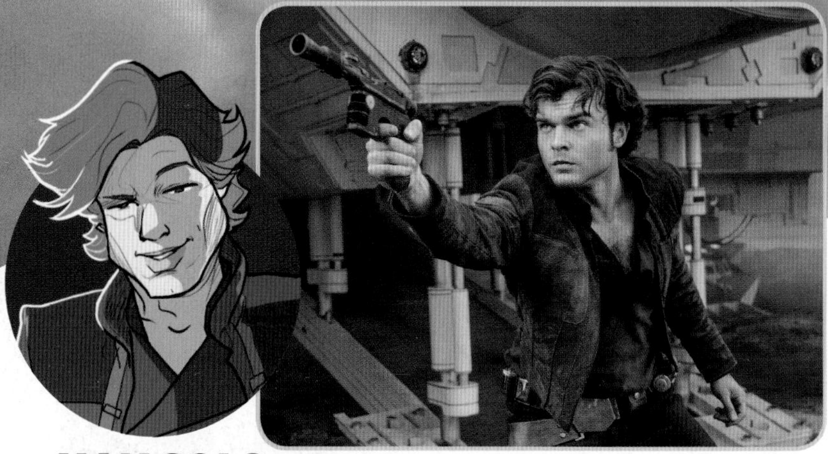

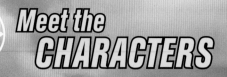

HAN SOLO

Being a scrumrat teaches you how to steal, bargain, fight, deceive, and trick your enemies, and do **whatever it takes to survive**—including betray your masters. Han has learned all these abilities during his involvement with the criminal organization the **White Worms** and is now determined to use them to gain what he desires the most: **freedom**... for himself and for Qi'ra, the woman he loves.

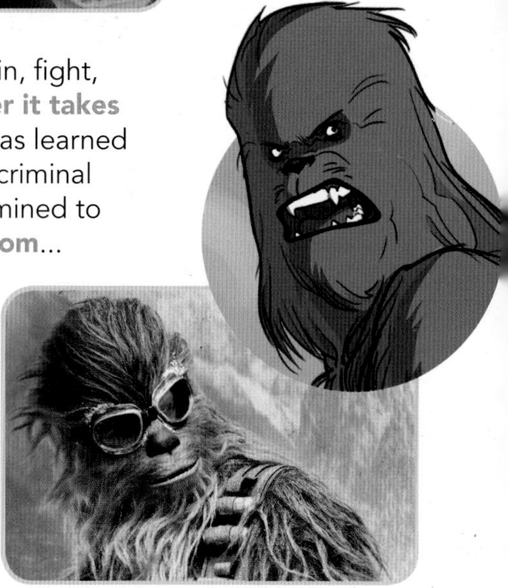

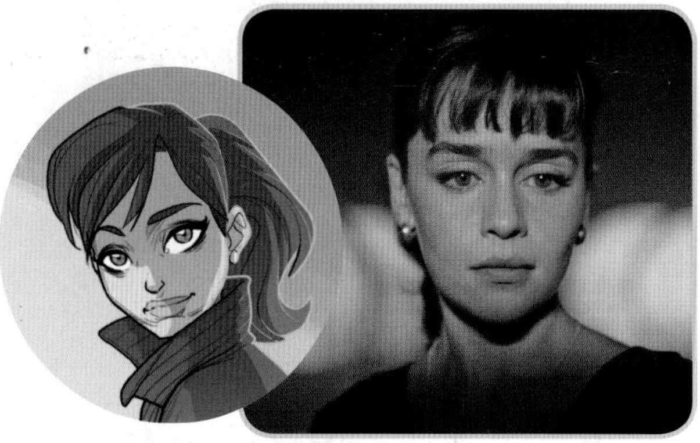

QI'RA

A street urchin like Han, Qi'ra shares his dream of a life of adventure and exploration. She hopes that one day they will find a way to **escape the criminal world**, but she is also keenly aware of how dangerous it could be. **Extremely practical**, Qi'ra believes in always having a plan.

CHEWBACCA

Scattered across the galaxy, hunted by the Empire, **most of the Wookiees have lost their freedom**. Chewbacca is being held in an underground cell on planet Mimban—where a war is raging between the Empire and the local resistance. **Called "the beast,"** Chewbacca is treated like an animal by his Imperial captors.

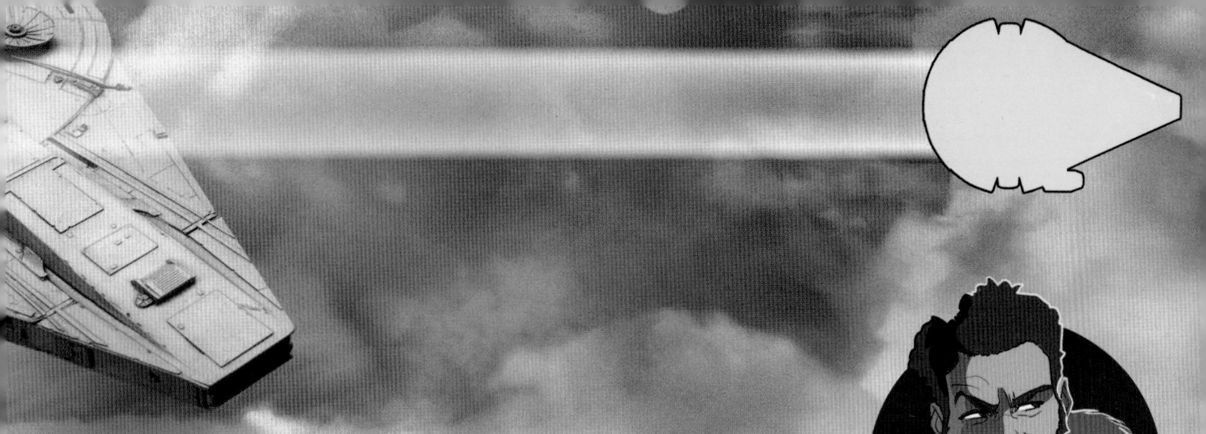

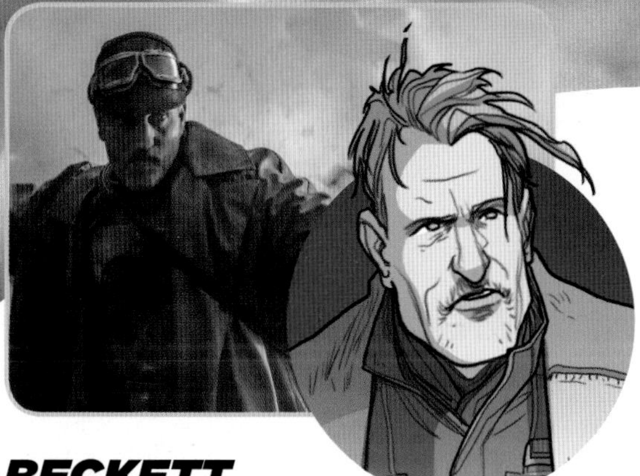

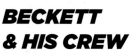

BECKETT & HIS CREW

A survivor, Tobias Beckett has been a **professional thief** for a long time and has learned not to trust anyone, except for **Val**—the woman he wants to spend his retirement days with—and **Rio**, an Ardennian with four arms and a talent for piloting. However, despite this, Beckett is occasionally willing to accept new members in his crew.

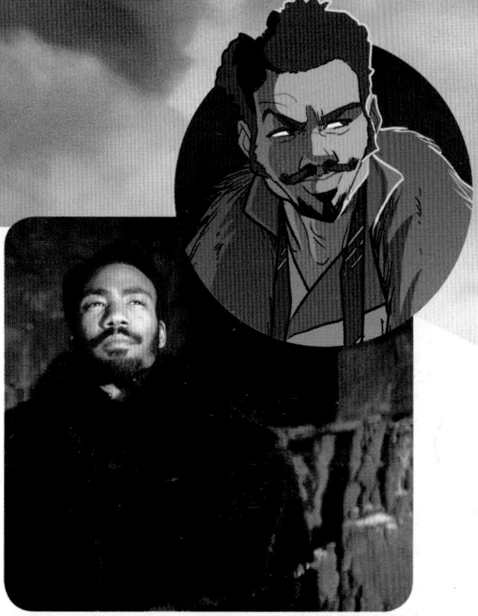

LANDO CALRISSIAN

Probably the **best smuggler around**, Lando Calrissian has slipped through the Empire's fingers more times than anyone alive, thanks to his charm, his cunning, and his customized YT-1300 starship, the ***Millennium Falcon***. A born gambler, Lando has won a lot of things, including a moon, at a card game called sabacc.

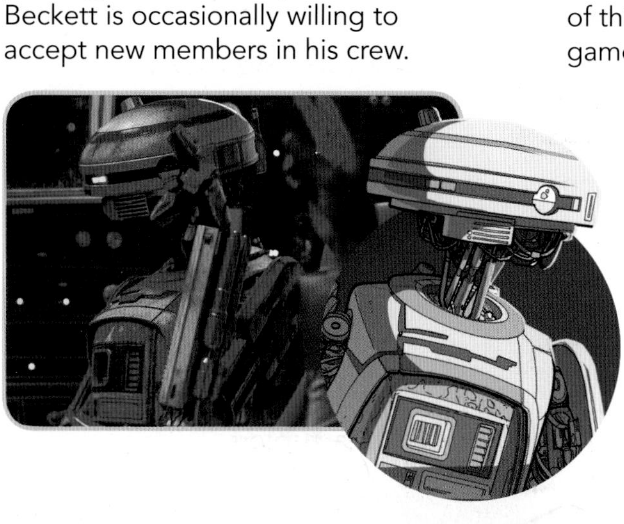

L3-37

Lando's first mate, who has the best navigational database in the galaxy, is unlike any other droid. **An advocate for droids' rights**, L3-37 believes they shouldn't always follow their programming, especially when their owners force them to fight against one another to amuse a crowd.

Meet the CHARACTERS

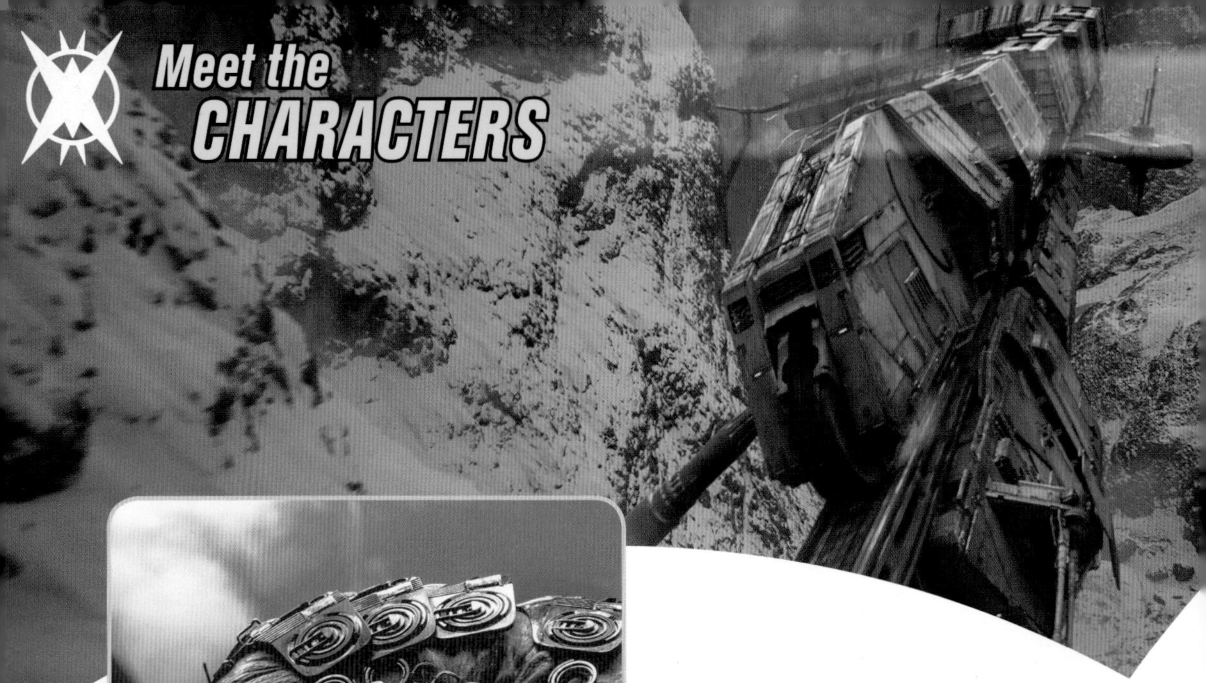

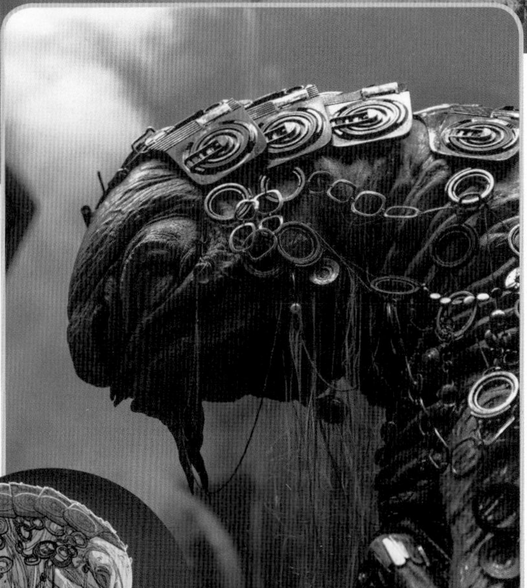

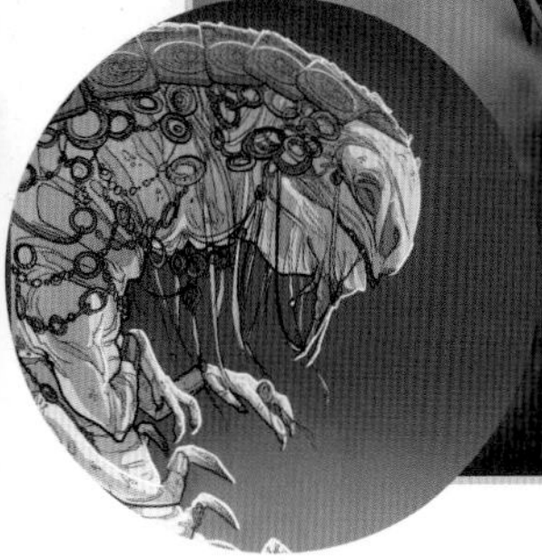

MOLOCH

Proxima's loyal lieutenant, Moloch makes sure all the scrumrats carry out their tasks and punishes those who fail without hesitation. Also **a Grindalid**, Moloch wears a mask that allows him to venture above the surface, protecting his skin from sunlight and filtering Corellia's dirty air.

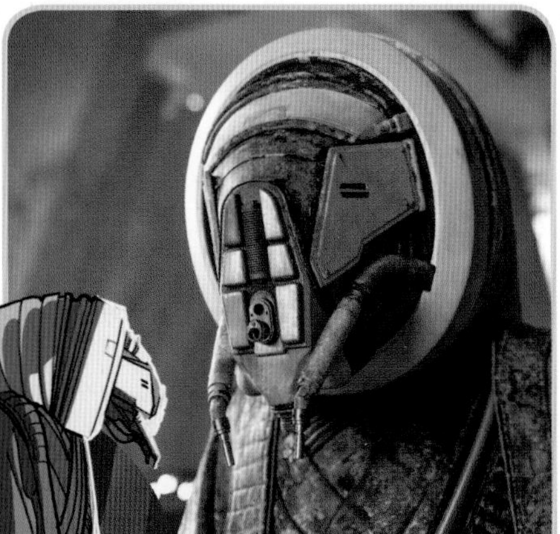

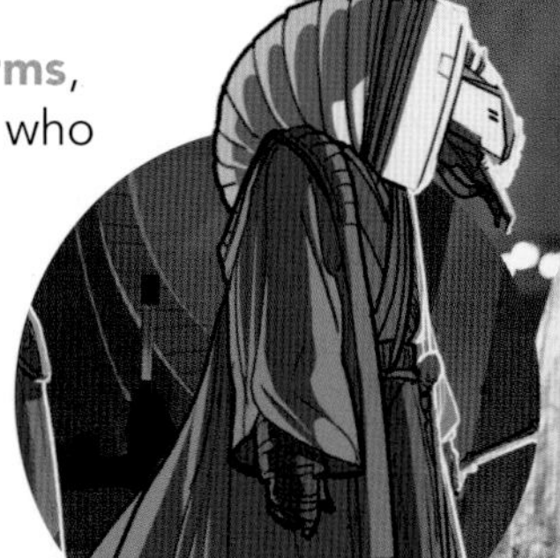

PROXIMA

The matriarch of the White Worms, Lady Proxima is a **merciless boss** who never forgives a failure. From the sewer tunnels beneath Corellia's Coronet City, Proxima sends her scrumrats to steal and bargain on her behalf. As **a Grindalid**, she must protect her skin against any source of light.

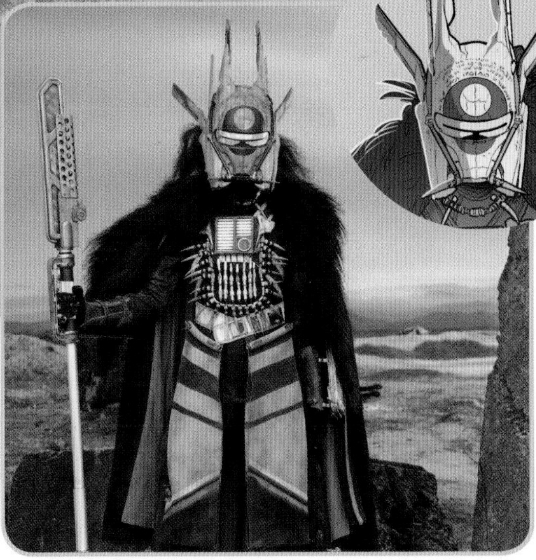

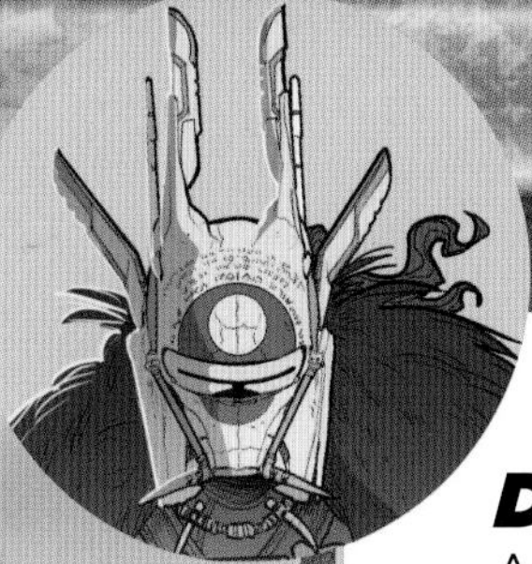

DRYDEN VOS

An essential member of the **Crimson Dawn crime syndicate**, Dryden Vos is a sophisticated and elegant gangster who **enjoys luxury and power** aboard his star yacht *First Light*. But he is also a master of the deadly hand-to-hand combat form known as Teräs Käsi and **a ruthless assassin** with very little patience for those who disappoint him.

ENFYS NEST

A pirate, a marauder, and a skillful warrior, Enfys Nest is above all else **a mystery**: no one knows who's hiding behind the mask and armor of this ferocious leader. Thieving from thieves, Enfys Nest and the other members of the Cloud-Riders swoop gang have become **a nightmare for criminals** like Beckett and Val.

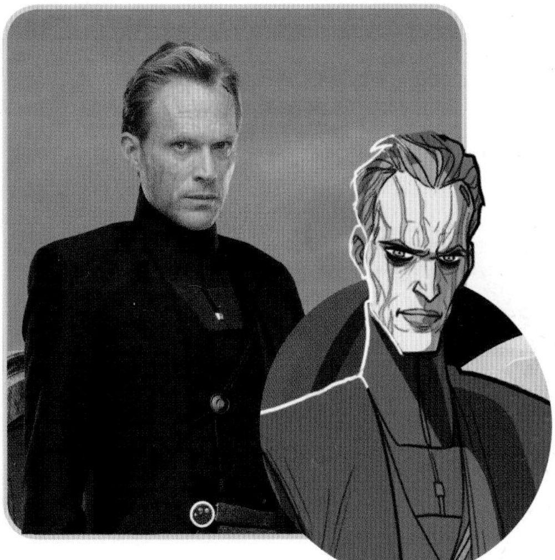

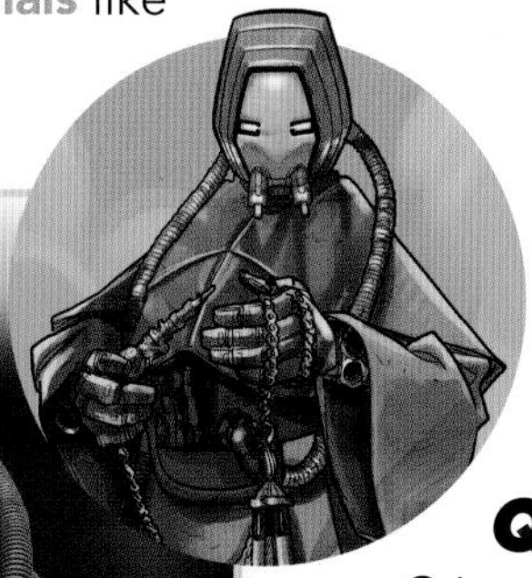

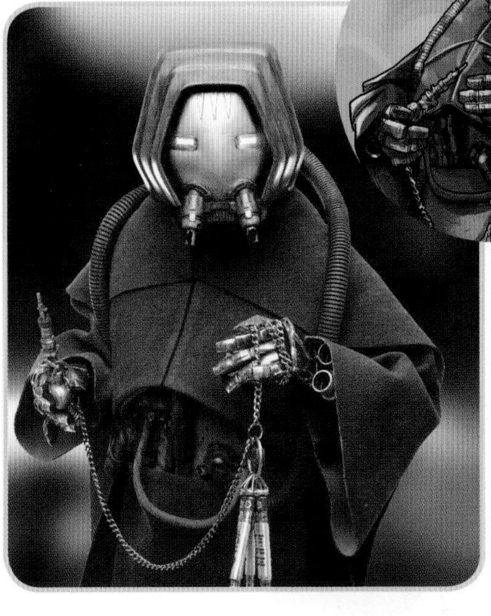

QUAY TOLSITE

Crimson Dawn isn't the only **crime organization tolerated by the Empire**. Another, the **Pyke Syndicate**, controls the colony of Kessel, where it extracts vast amounts of spice and coaxium—a highly valuable hyperfuel. Administering the Kessel site is Quay Tolsite, a **cruel director of operations** who employs slaves, especially Wookiees, as miners.

"WE GET OUR OWN SHIP, GO ANYWHERE WE WANT, AND NEVER HAVE TO TAKE ORDERS OR BE KICKED AROUND BY ANYBODY."

QI'RA

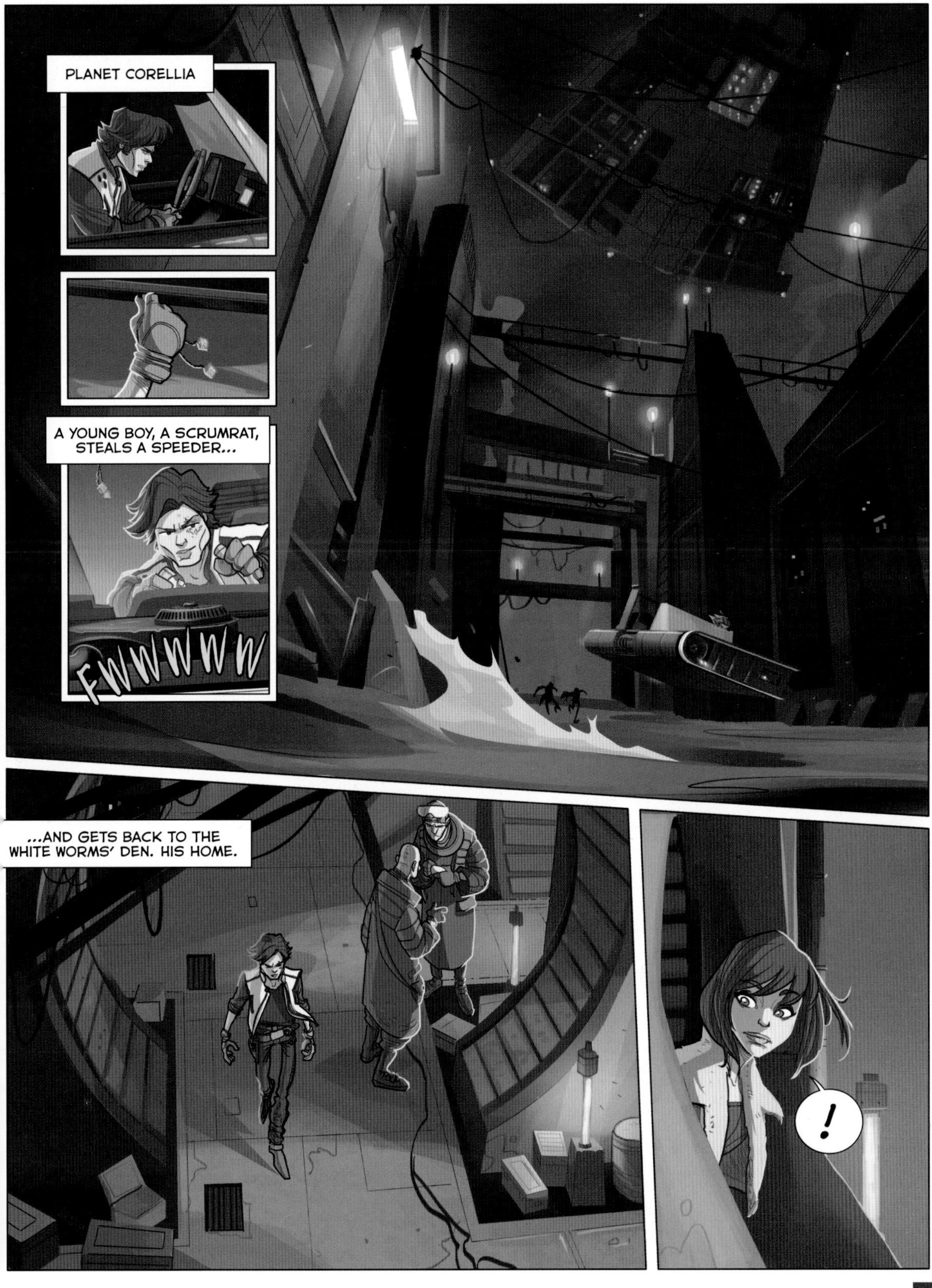
PLANET CORELLIA
A YOUNG BOY, A SCRUMRAT, STEALS A SPEEDER...
FWWWWW
...AND GETS BACK TO THE WHITE WORMS' DEN. HIS HOME.
!

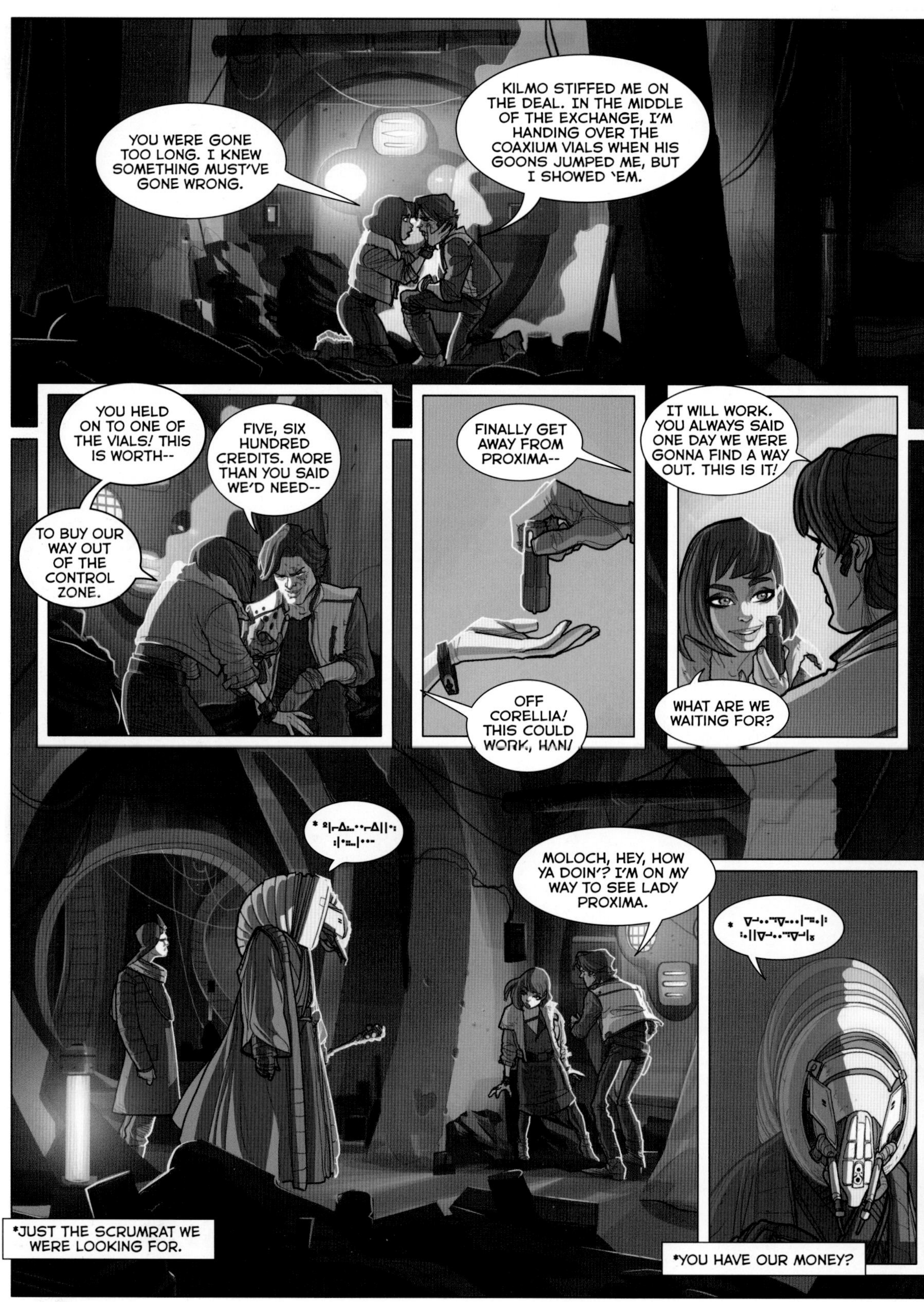
YOU WERE GONE TOO LONG. I KNEW SOMETHING MUST'VE GONE WRONG.
KILMO STIFFED ME ON THE DEAL. IN THE MIDDLE OF THE EXCHANGE, I'M HANDING OVER THE COAXIUM VIALS WHEN HIS GOONS JUMPED ME, BUT I SHOWED 'EM.
YOU HELD ON TO ONE OF THE VIALS! THIS IS WORTH--
FIVE, SIX HUNDRED CREDITS. MORE THAN YOU SAID WE'D NEED--
TO BUY OUR WAY OUT OF THE CONTROL ZONE.
FINALLY GET AWAY FROM PROXIMA--
OFF CORELLIA! THIS COULD WORK, HAN!
IT WILL WORK. YOU ALWAYS SAID ONE DAY WE WERE GONNA FIND A WAY OUT. THIS IS IT!
WHAT ARE WE WAITING FOR?
*JUST THE SCRUMRAT WE WERE LOOKING FOR.
MOLOCH, HEY, HOW YA DOIN'? I'M ON MY WAY TO SEE LADY PROXIMA.
*YOU HAVE OUR MONEY?

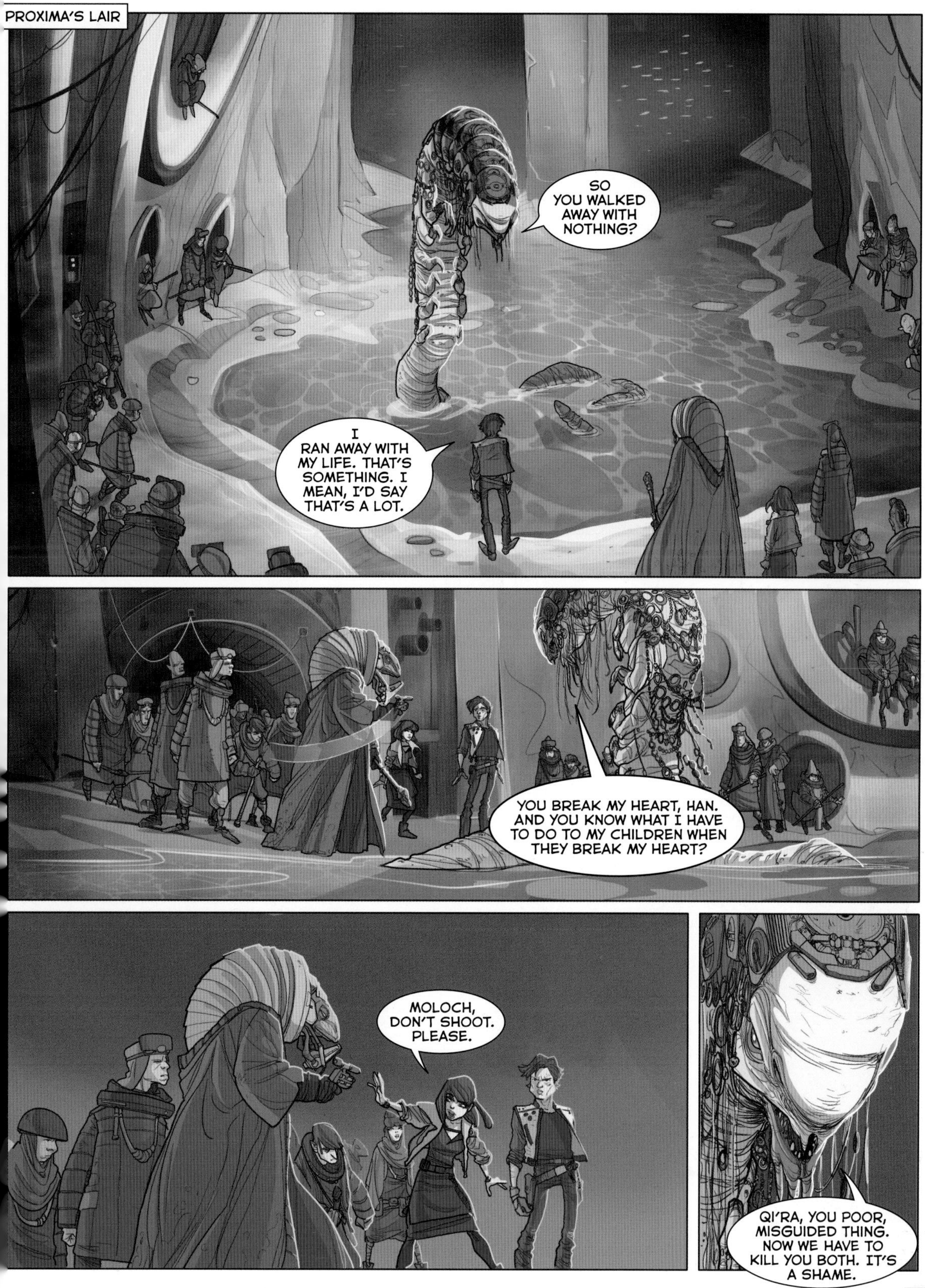

PROXIMA'S LAIR
SO YOU WALKED AWAY WITH NOTHING?
I RAN AWAY WITH MY LIFE. THAT'S SOMETHING. I MEAN, I'D SAY THAT'S A LOT.
YOU BREAK MY HEART, HAN. AND YOU KNOW WHAT I HAVE TO DO TO MY CHILDREN WHEN THEY BREAK MY HEART?
MOLOCH, DON'T SHOOT. PLEASE.
QI'RA, YOU POOR, MISGUIDED THING. NOW WE HAVE TO KILL YOU BOTH. IT'S A SHAME.

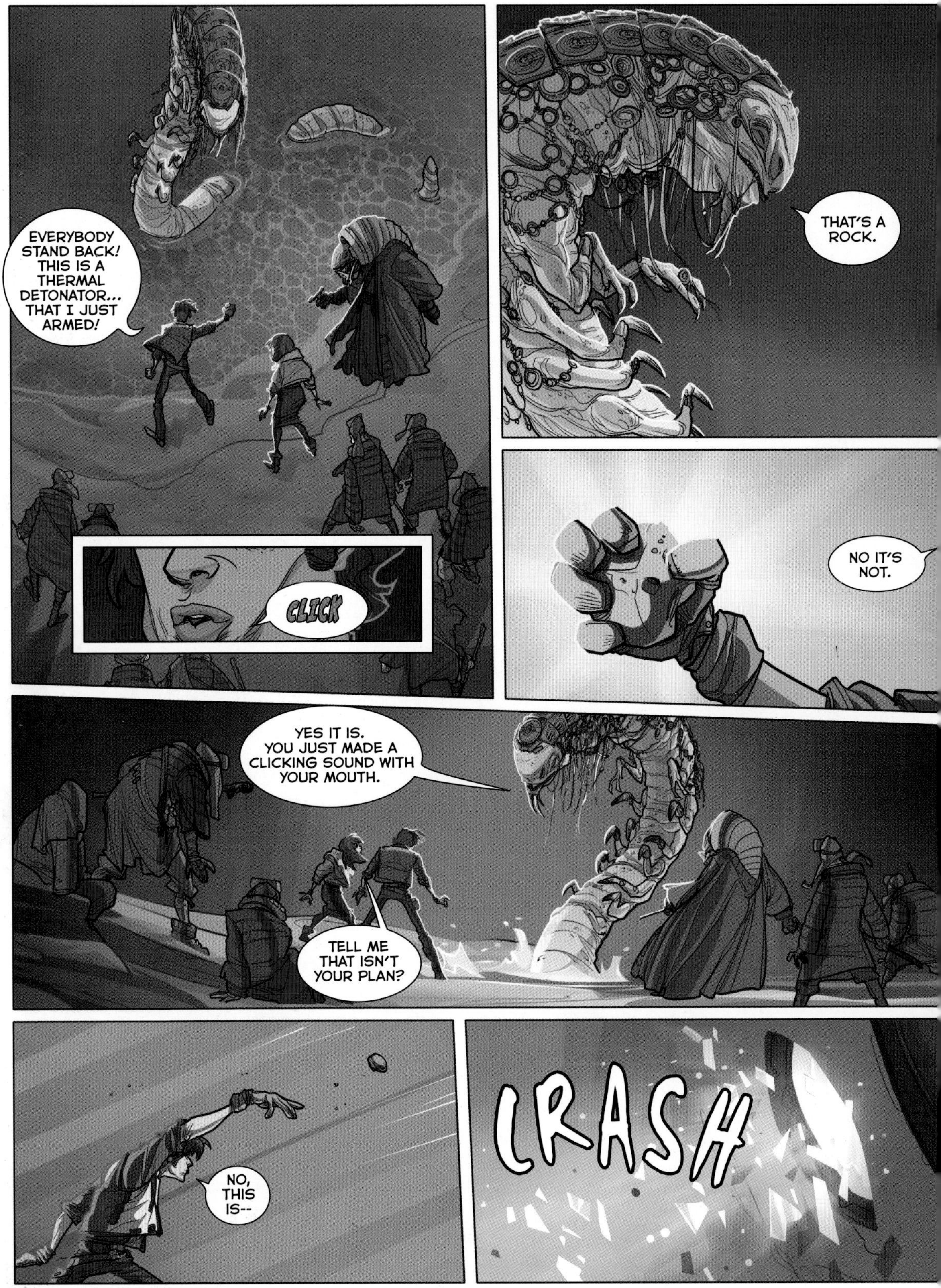

EVERYBODY STAND BACK! THIS IS A THERMAL DETONATOR... THAT I JUST ARMED!
CLICK
THAT'S A ROCK.
NO IT'S NOT.
YES IT IS. YOU JUST MADE A CLICKING SOUND WITH YOUR MOUTH.
TELL ME THAT ISN'T YOUR PLAN?
NO, THIS IS--
CRASH

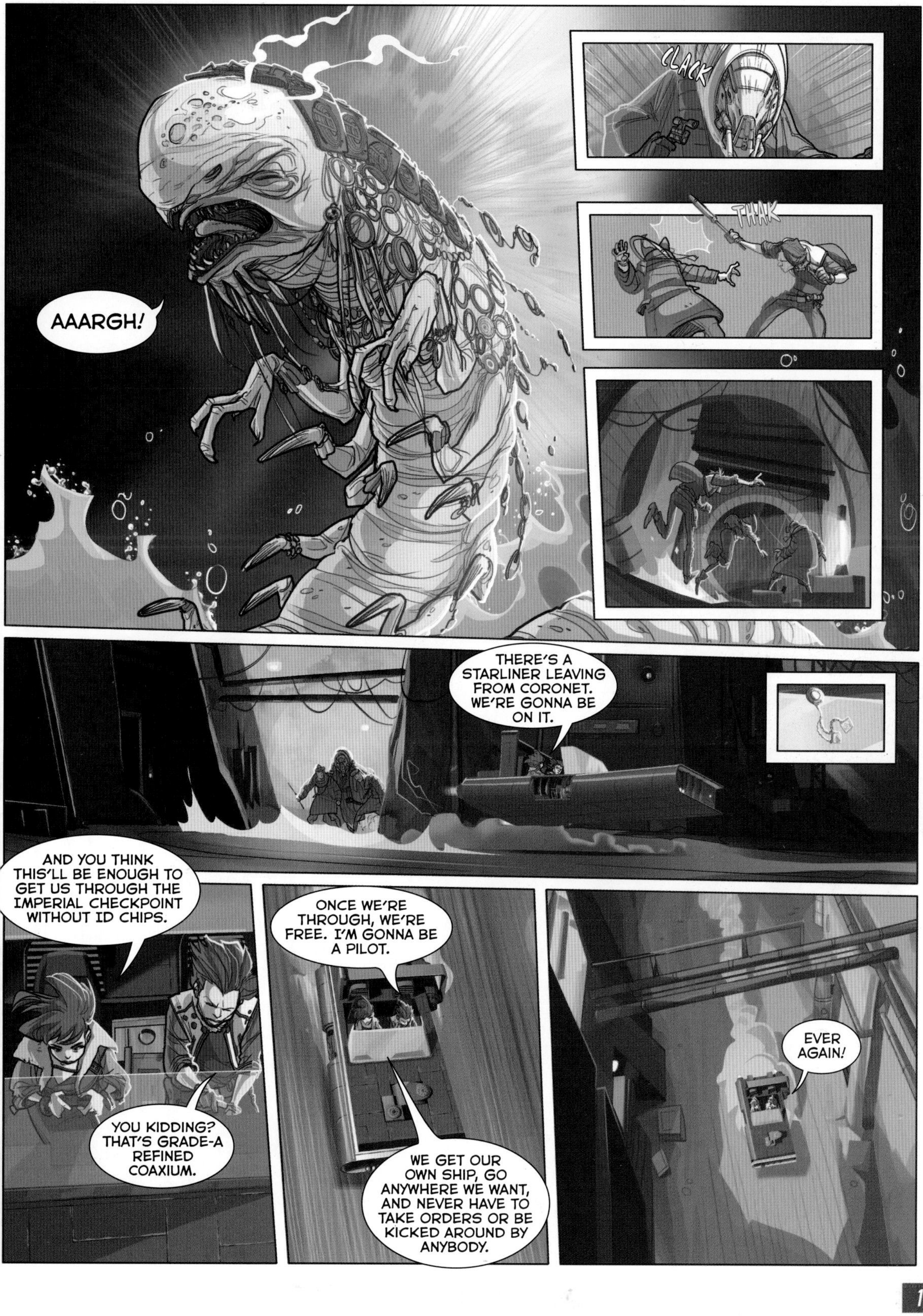
CLACK
THAK
AAARGH!
THERE'S A STARLINER LEAVING FROM CORONET. WE'RE GONNA BE ON IT.
AND YOU THINK THIS'LL BE ENOUGH TO GET US THROUGH THE IMPERIAL CHECKPOINT WITHOUT ID CHIPS.
YOU KIDDING? THAT'S GRADE-A REFINED COAXIUM.
ONCE WE'RE THROUGH, WE'RE FREE. I'M GONNA BE A PILOT.
WE GET OUR OWN SHIP, GO ANYWHERE WE WANT, AND NEVER HAVE TO TAKE ORDERS OR BE KICKED AROUND BY ANYBODY.
EVER AGAIN!

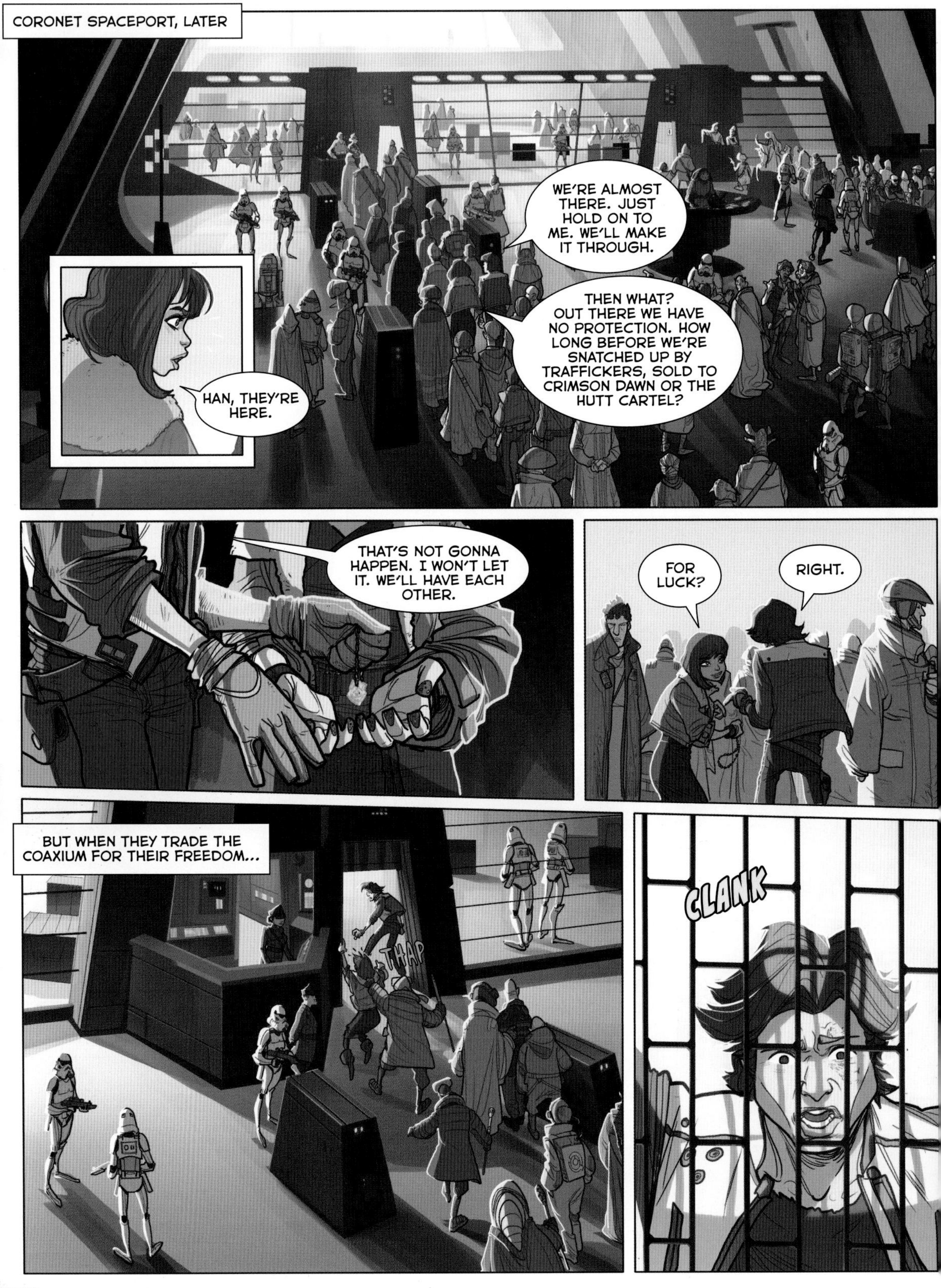
CORONET SPACEPORT, LATER
HAN, THEY'RE HERE.
WE'RE ALMOST THERE. JUST HOLD ON TO ME. WE'LL MAKE IT THROUGH.
THEN WHAT? OUT THERE WE HAVE NO PROTECTION. HOW LONG BEFORE WE'RE SNATCHED UP BY TRAFFICKERS, SOLD TO CRIMSON DAWN OR THE HUTT CARTEL?
THAT'S NOT GONNA HAPPEN. I WON'T LET IT. WE'LL HAVE EACH OTHER.
FOR LUCK?
RIGHT.
BUT WHEN THEY TRADE THE COAXIUM FOR THEIR FREEDOM...
THAP
CLANK

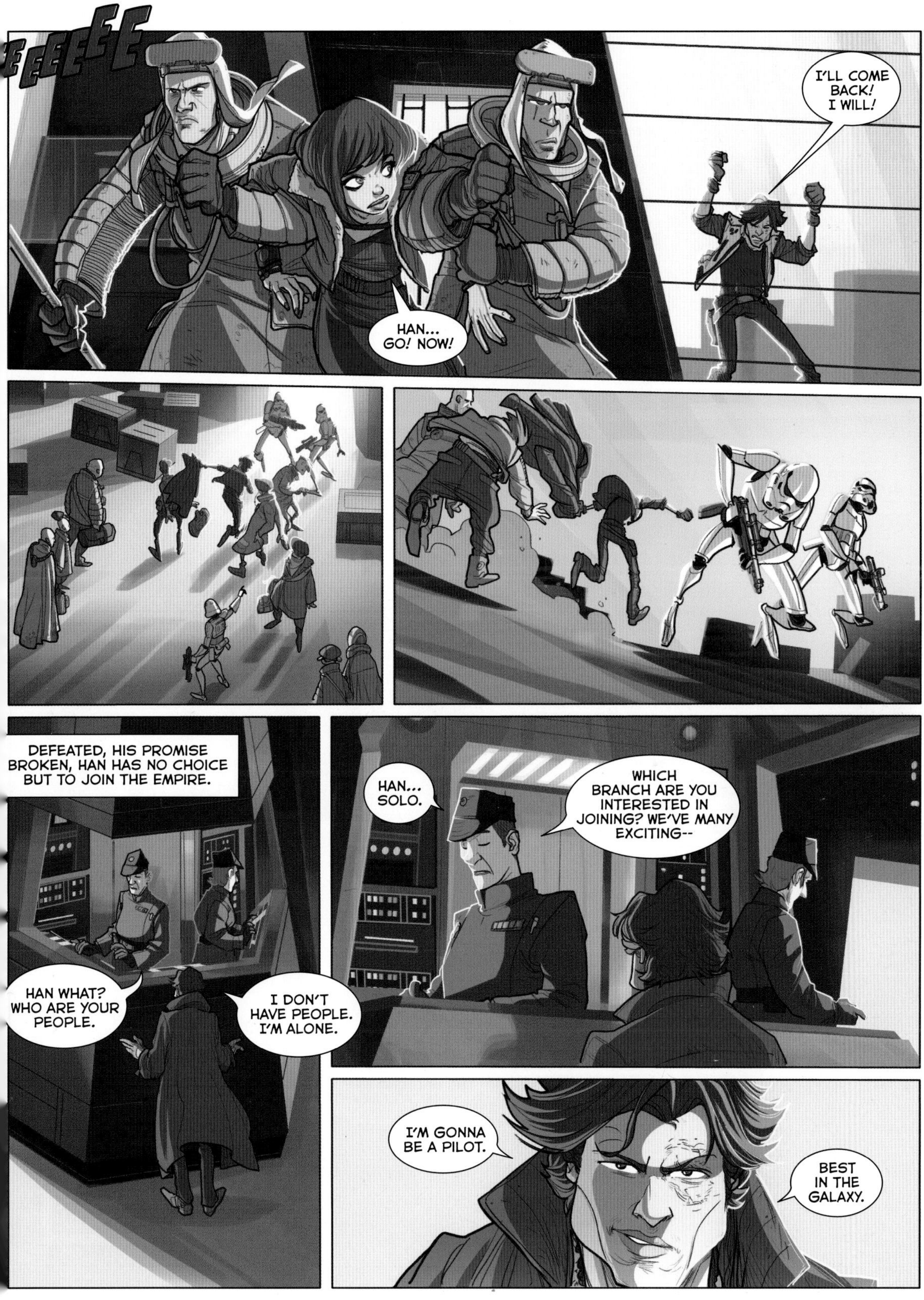
EEEEEE
HAN... GO! NOW!
I'LL COME BACK! I WILL!
DEFEATED, HIS PROMISE BROKEN, HAN HAS NO CHOICE BUT TO JOIN THE EMPIRE.
HAN WHAT? WHO ARE YOUR PEOPLE.
I DON'T HAVE PEOPLE. I'M ALONE.
HAN... SOLO.
WHICH BRANCH ARE YOU INTERESTED IN JOINING? WE'VE MANY EXCITING--
I'M GONNA BE A PILOT.
BEST IN THE GALAXY.

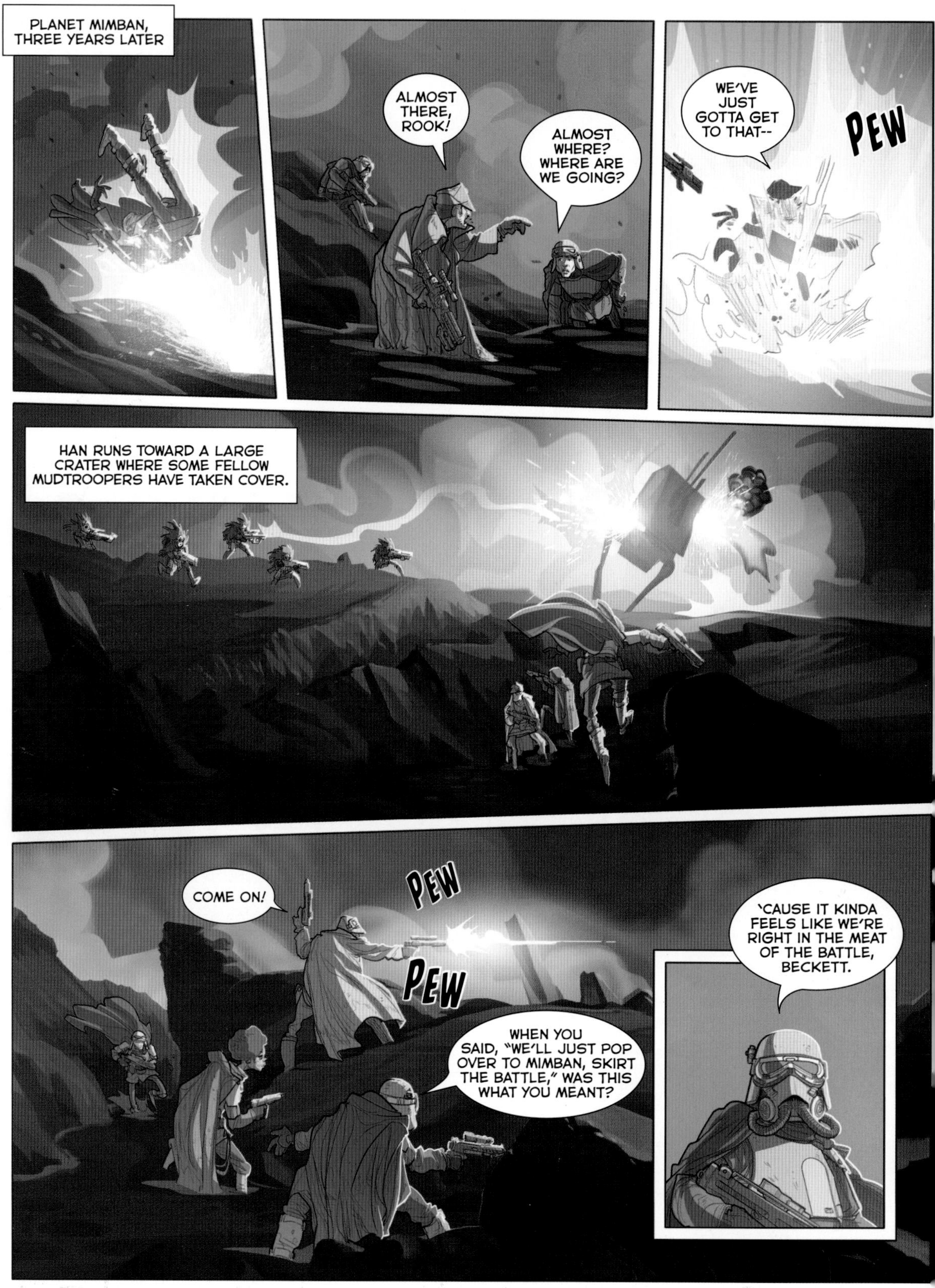
PLANET MIMBAN, THREE YEARS LATER
ALMOST THERE, ROOK!
ALMOST WHERE? WHERE ARE WE GOING?
WE'VE JUST GOTTA GET TO THAT--
PEW
HAN RUNS TOWARD A LARGE CRATER WHERE SOME FELLOW MUDTROOPERS HAVE TAKEN COVER.
COME ON!
PEW
PEW
WHEN YOU SAID, "WE'LL JUST POP OVER TO MIMBAN, SKIRT THE BATTLE," WAS THIS WHAT YOU MEANT?
'CAUSE IT KINDA FEELS LIKE WE'RE RIGHT IN THE MEAT OF THE BATTLE, BECKETT.

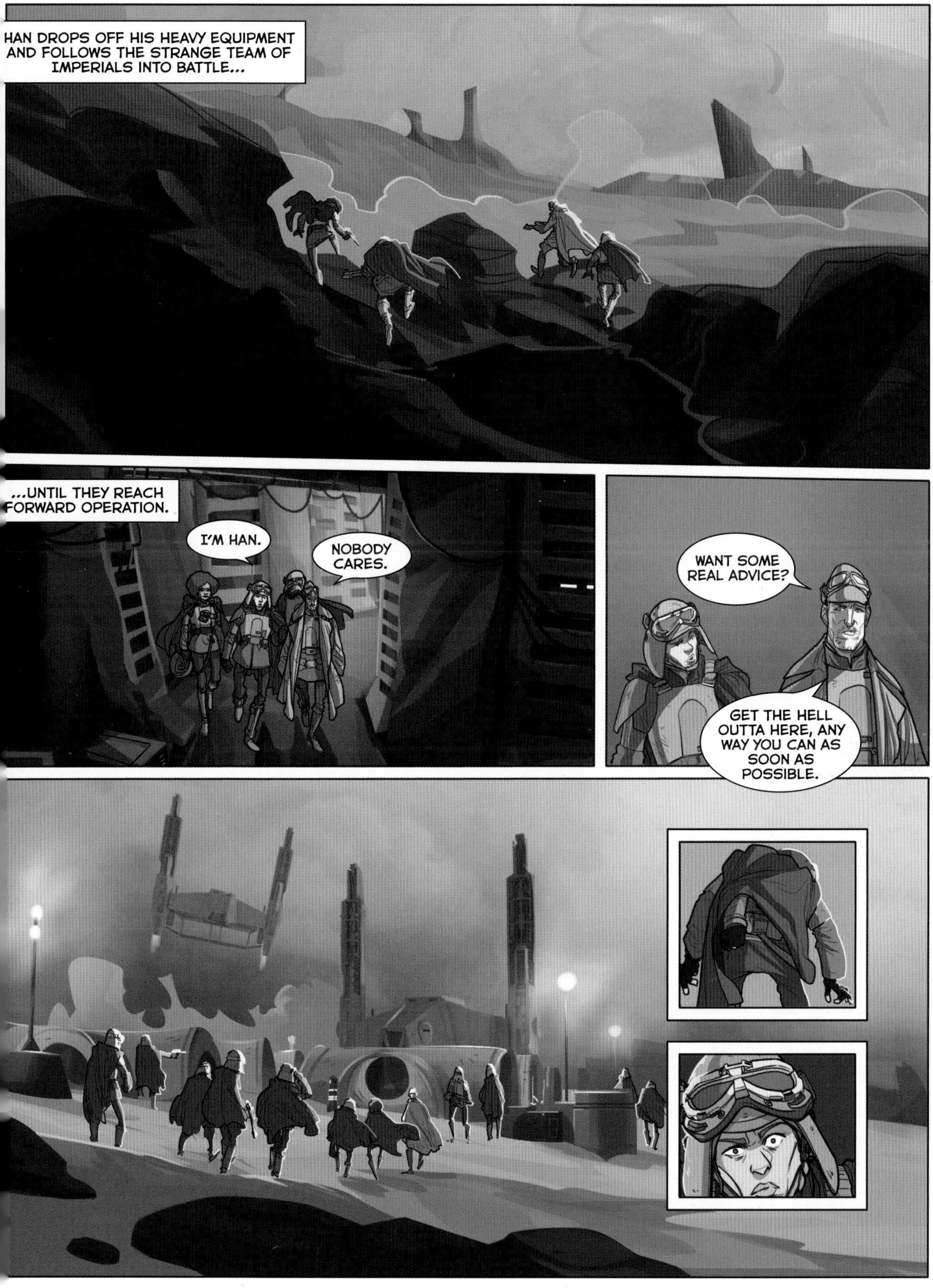

HAN DROPS OFF HIS HEAVY EQUIPMENT AND FOLLOWS THE STRANGE TEAM OF IMPERIALS INTO BATTLE...
...UNTIL THEY REACH FORWARD OPERATION.
I'M HAN.
NOBODY CARES.
WANT SOME REAL ADVICE?
GET THE HELL OUTTA HERE, ANY WAY YOU CAN AS SOON AS POSSIBLE.

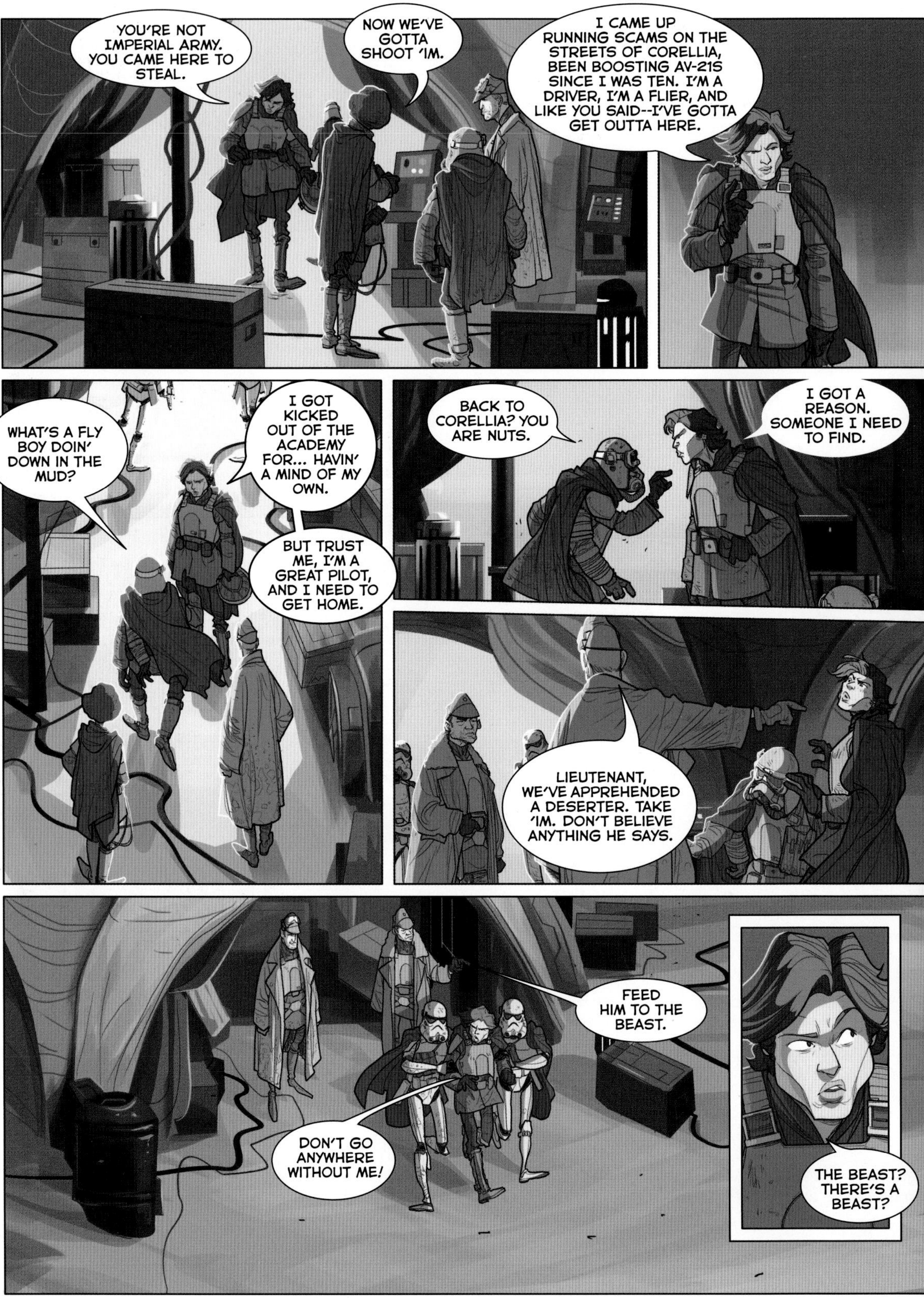
YOU'RE NOT IMPERIAL ARMY. YOU CAME HERE TO STEAL.
NOW WE'VE GOTTA SHOOT 'IM.
I CAME UP RUNNING SCAMS ON THE STREETS OF CORELLIA, BEEN BOOSTING AV-21S SINCE I WAS TEN. I'M A DRIVER, I'M A FLIER, AND LIKE YOU SAID--I'VE GOTTA GET OUTTA HERE.
WHAT'S A FLY BOY DOIN' DOWN IN THE MUD?
I GOT KICKED OUT OF THE ACADEMY FOR... HAVIN' A MIND OF MY OWN.
BUT TRUST ME, I'M A GREAT PILOT, AND I NEED TO GET HOME.
BACK TO CORELLIA? YOU ARE NUTS.
I GOT A REASON. SOMEONE I NEED TO FIND.
LIEUTENANT, WE'VE APPREHENDED A DESERTER. TAKE 'IM. DON'T BELIEVE ANYTHING HE SAYS.
FEED HIM TO THE BEAST.
DON'T GO ANYWHERE WITHOUT ME!
THE BEAST? THERE'S A BEAST?

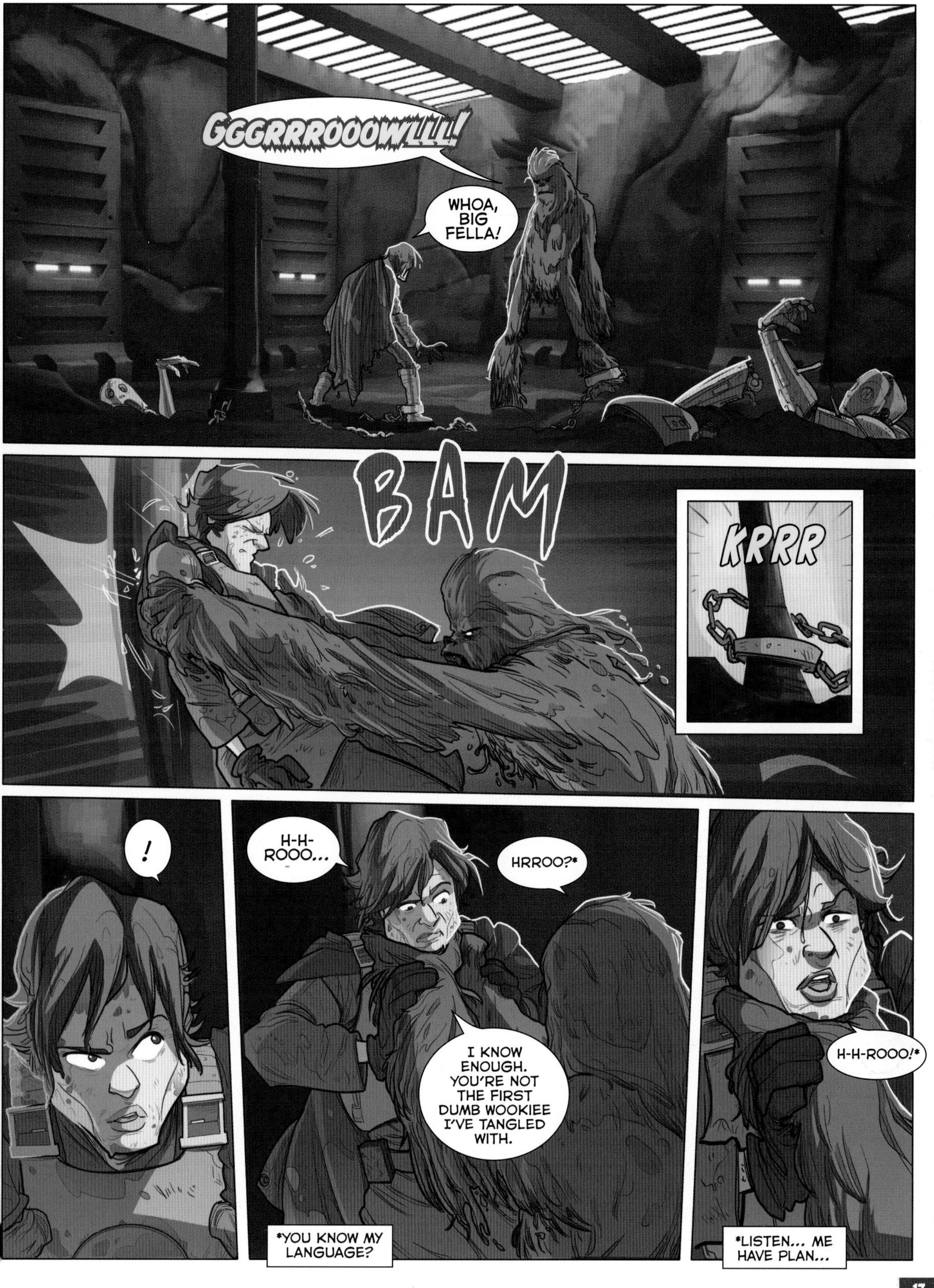
GGGRRROOOWLLL!
WHOA, BIG FELLA!
BAM
KRRR
!
H-H-ROOO...
HRROO?*
I KNOW ENOUGH. YOU'RE NOT THE FIRST DUMB WOOKIEE I'VE TANGLED WITH.
*YOU KNOW MY LANGUAGE?
H-H-ROOO!*
*LISTEN... ME HAVE PLAN...

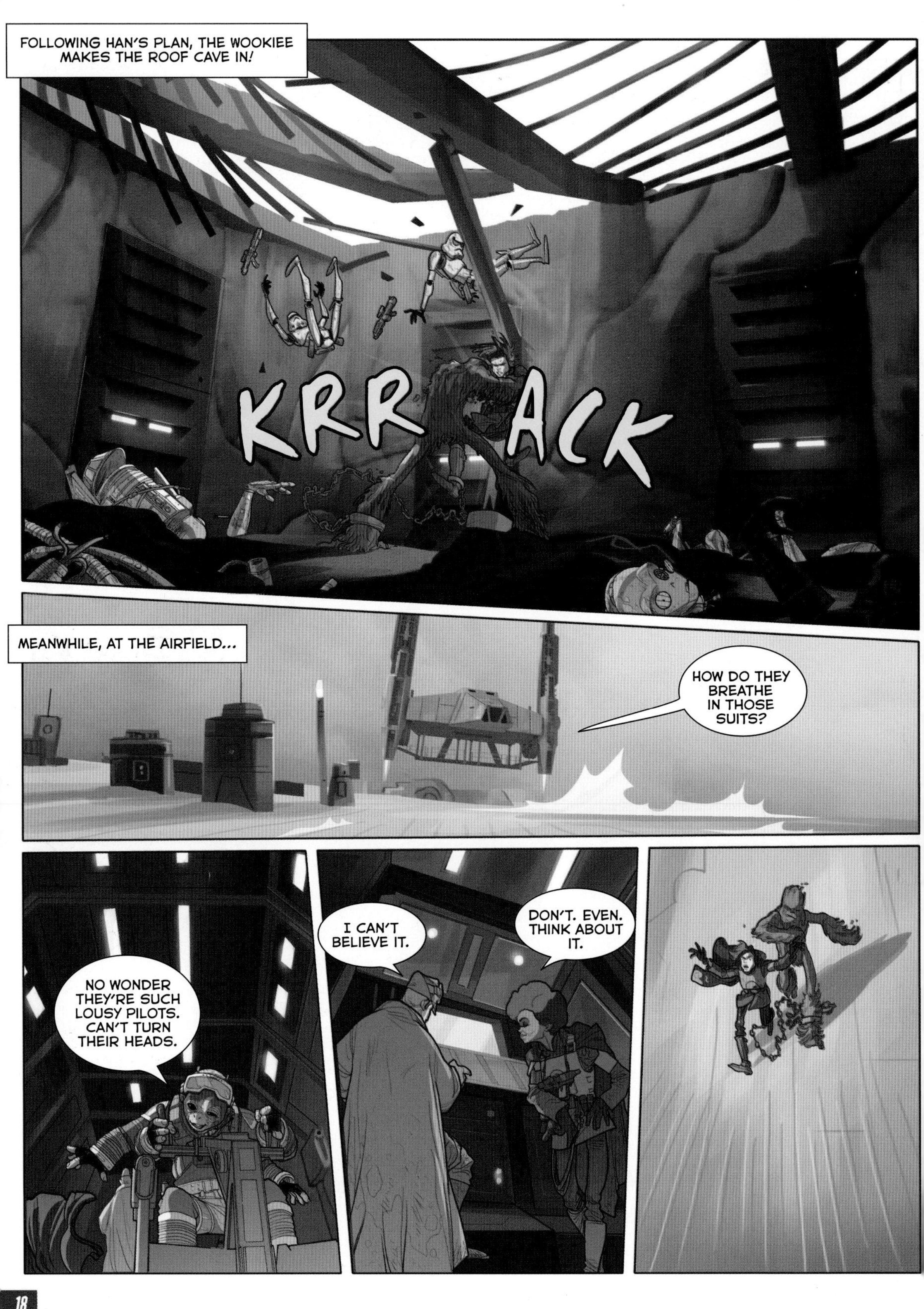
FOLLOWING HAN'S PLAN, THE WOOKIEE MAKES THE ROOF CAVE IN!
KRRACK
MEANWHILE, AT THE AIRFIELD...
HOW DO THEY BREATHE IN THOSE SUITS?
NO WONDER THEY'RE SUCH LOUSY PILOTS. CAN'T TURN THEIR HEADS.
I CAN'T BELIEVE IT.
DON'T. EVEN. THINK ABOUT IT.

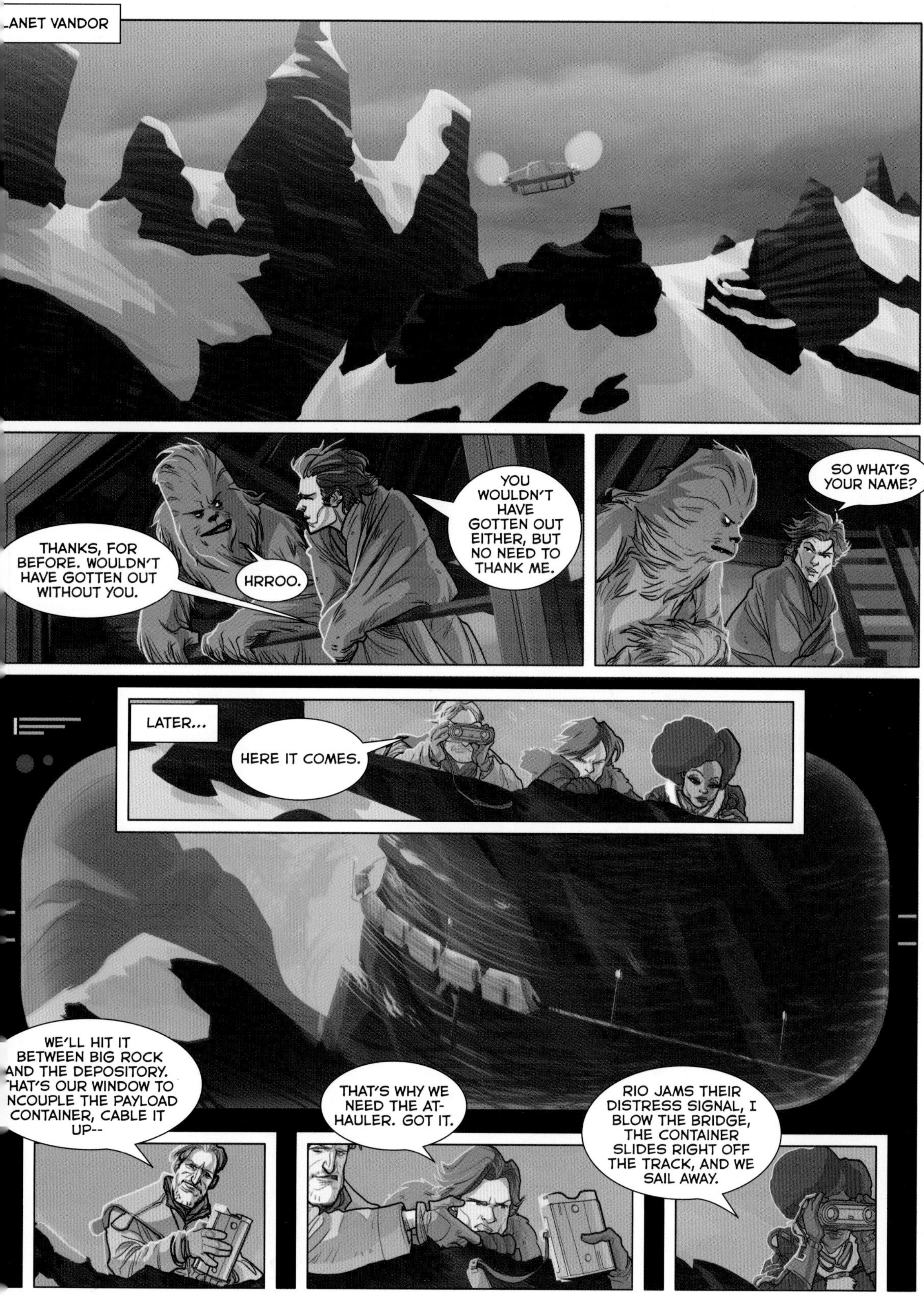

LANET VANDOR
THANKS, FOR BEFORE. WOULDN'T HAVE GOTTEN OUT WITHOUT YOU.
HRROO.
YOU WOULDN'T HAVE GOTTEN OUT EITHER, BUT NO NEED TO THANK ME.
SO WHAT'S YOUR NAME?
LATER...
HERE IT COMES.
WE'LL HIT IT BETWEEN BIG ROCK AND THE DEPOSITORY. THAT'S OUR WINDOW TO NCOUPLE THE PAYLOAD CONTAINER, CABLE IT UP--
THAT'S WHY WE NEED THE AT-HAULER. GOT IT.
RIO JAMS THEIR DISTRESS SIGNAL, I BLOW THE BRIDGE, THE CONTAINER SLIDES RIGHT OFF THE TRACK, AND WE SAIL AWAY.

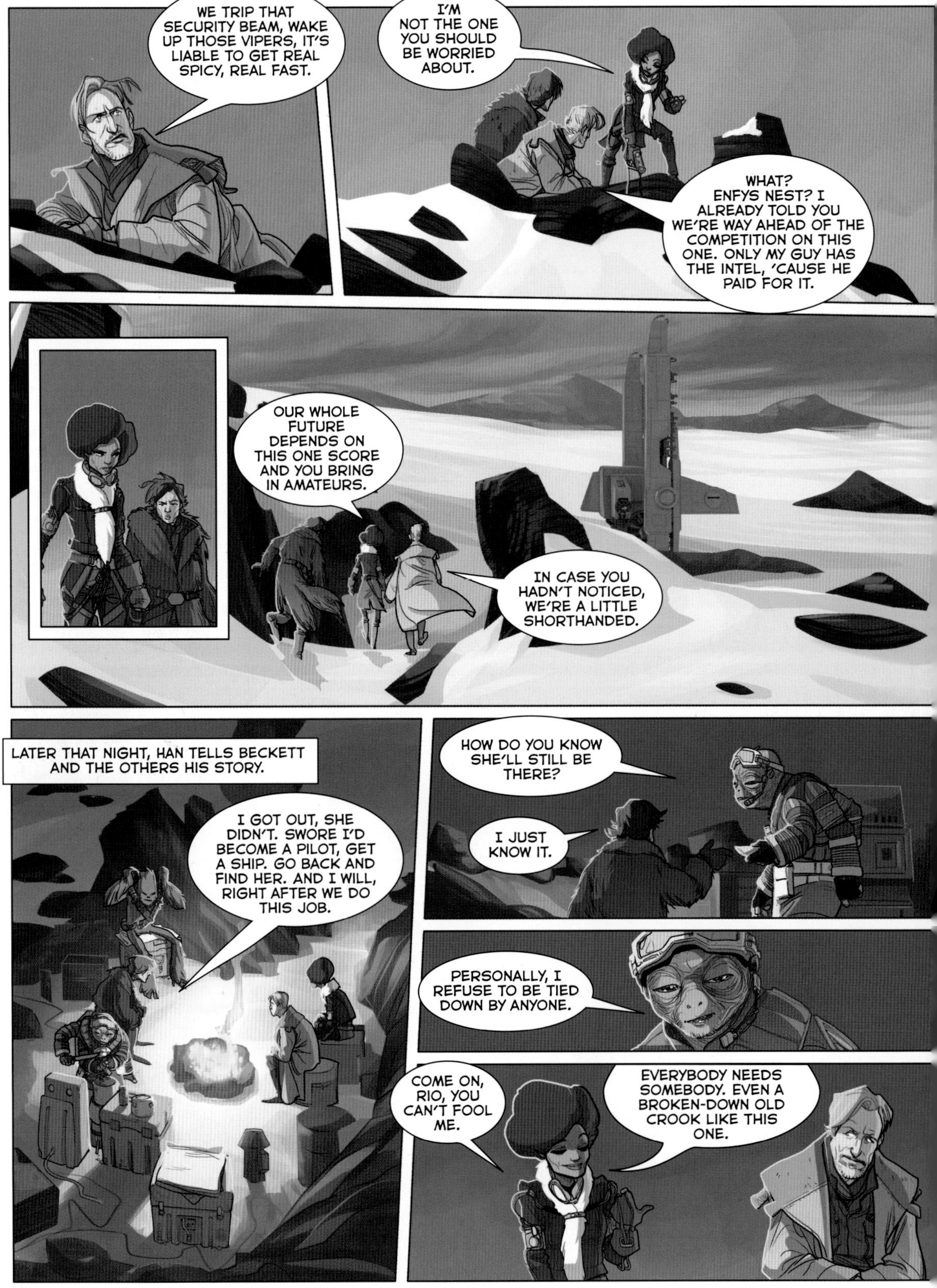
WE TRIP THAT SECURITY BEAM, WAKE UP THOSE VIPERS, IT'S LIABLE TO GET REAL SPICY, REAL FAST.
I'M NOT THE ONE YOU SHOULD BE WORRIED ABOUT.
WHAT? ENFYS NEST? I ALREADY TOLD YOU WE'RE WAY AHEAD OF THE COMPETITION ON THIS ONE. ONLY MY GUY HAS THE INTEL, 'CAUSE HE PAID FOR IT.
OUR WHOLE FUTURE DEPENDS ON THIS ONE SCORE AND YOU BRING IN AMATEURS.
IN CASE YOU HADN'T NOTICED, WE'RE A LITTLE SHORTHANDED.
LATER THAT NIGHT, HAN TELLS BECKETT AND THE OTHERS HIS STORY.
I GOT OUT, SHE DIDN'T. SWORE I'D BECOME A PILOT, GET A SHIP. GO BACK AND FIND HER. AND I WILL, RIGHT AFTER WE DO THIS JOB.
HOW DO YOU KNOW SHE'LL STILL BE THERE?
I JUST KNOW IT.
PERSONALLY, I REFUSE TO BE TIED DOWN BY ANYONE.
COME ON, RIO, YOU CAN'T FOOL ME.
EVERYBODY NEEDS SOMEBODY. EVEN A BROKEN-DOWN OLD CROOK LIKE THIS ONE.

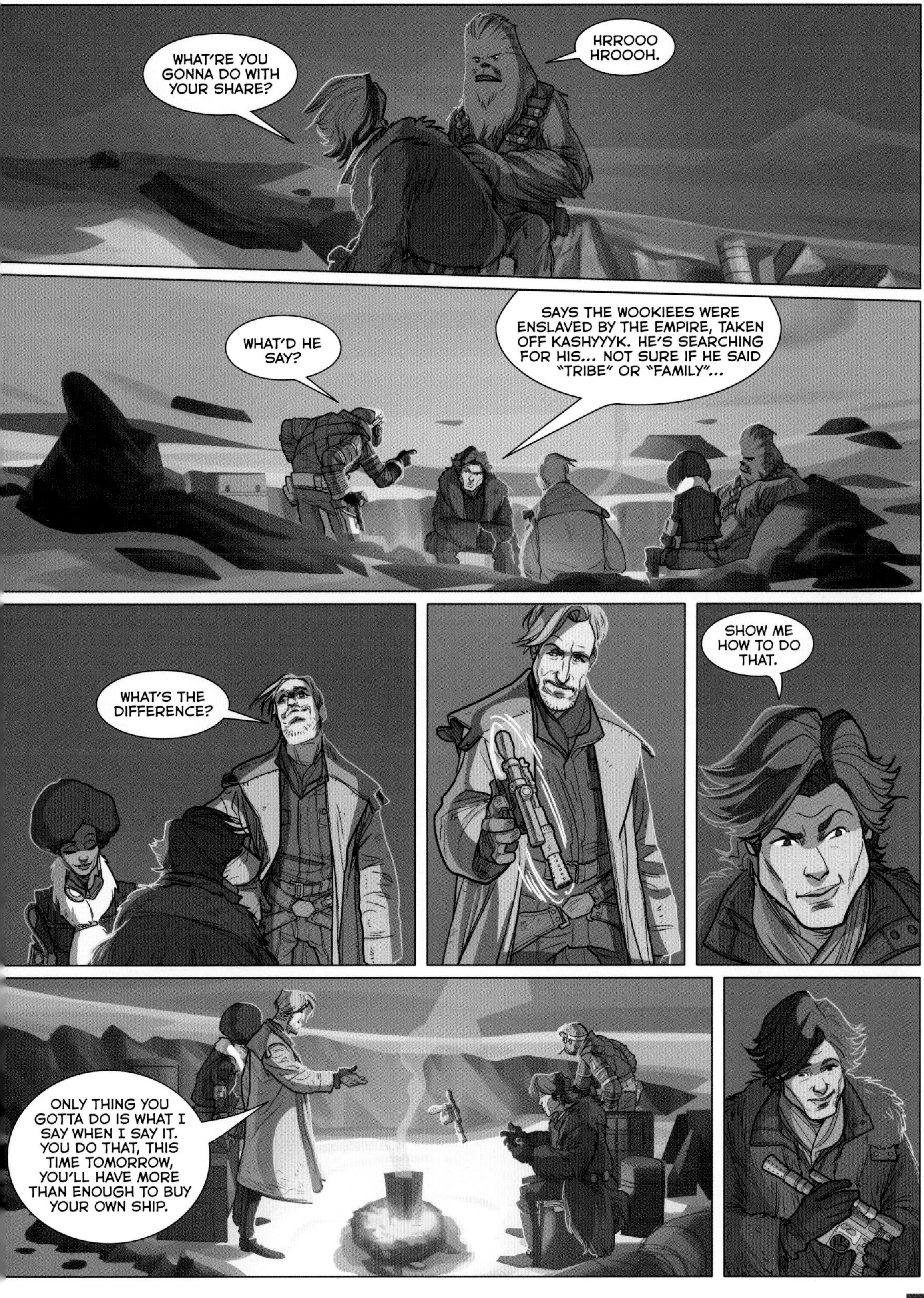
WHAT'RE YOU GONNA DO WITH YOUR SHARE?
HRROOO HROOOH.
WHAT'D HE SAY?
SAYS THE WOOKIEES WERE ENSLAVED BY THE EMPIRE, TAKEN OFF KASHYYYK. HE'S SEARCHING FOR HIS... NOT SURE IF HE SAID "TRIBE" OR "FAMILY"...
WHAT'S THE DIFFERENCE?
SHOW ME HOW TO DO THAT.
ONLY THING YOU GOTTA DO IS WHAT I SAY WHEN I SAY IT. YOU DO THAT, THIS TIME TOMORROW, YOU'LL HAVE MORE THAN ENOUGH TO BUY YOUR OWN SHIP.

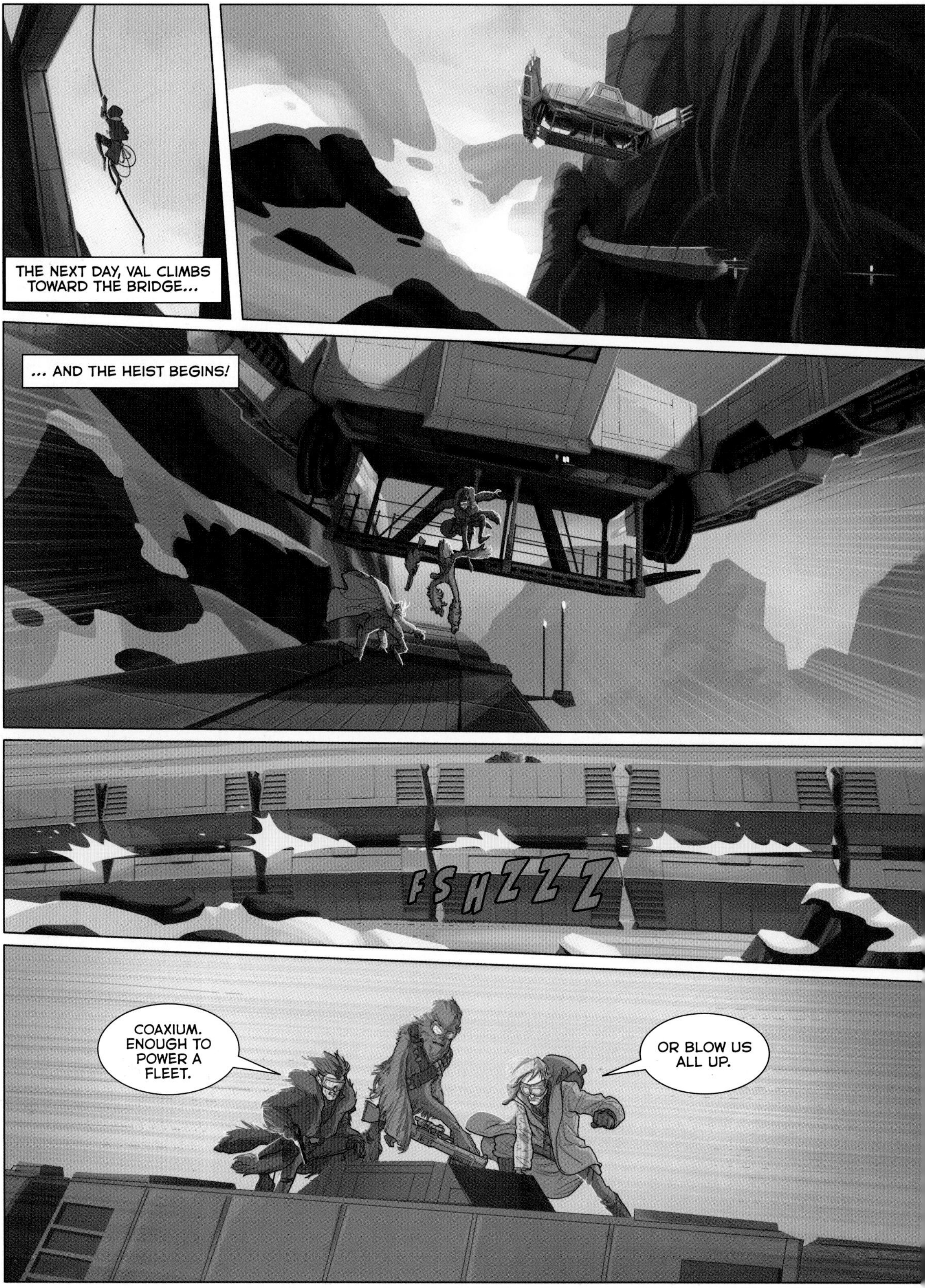
THE NEXT DAY, VAL CLIMBS TOWARD THE BRIDGE...
... AND THE HEIST BEGINS!
FSHZZZ
COAXIUM. ENOUGH TO POWER A FLEET.
OR BLOW US ALL UP.

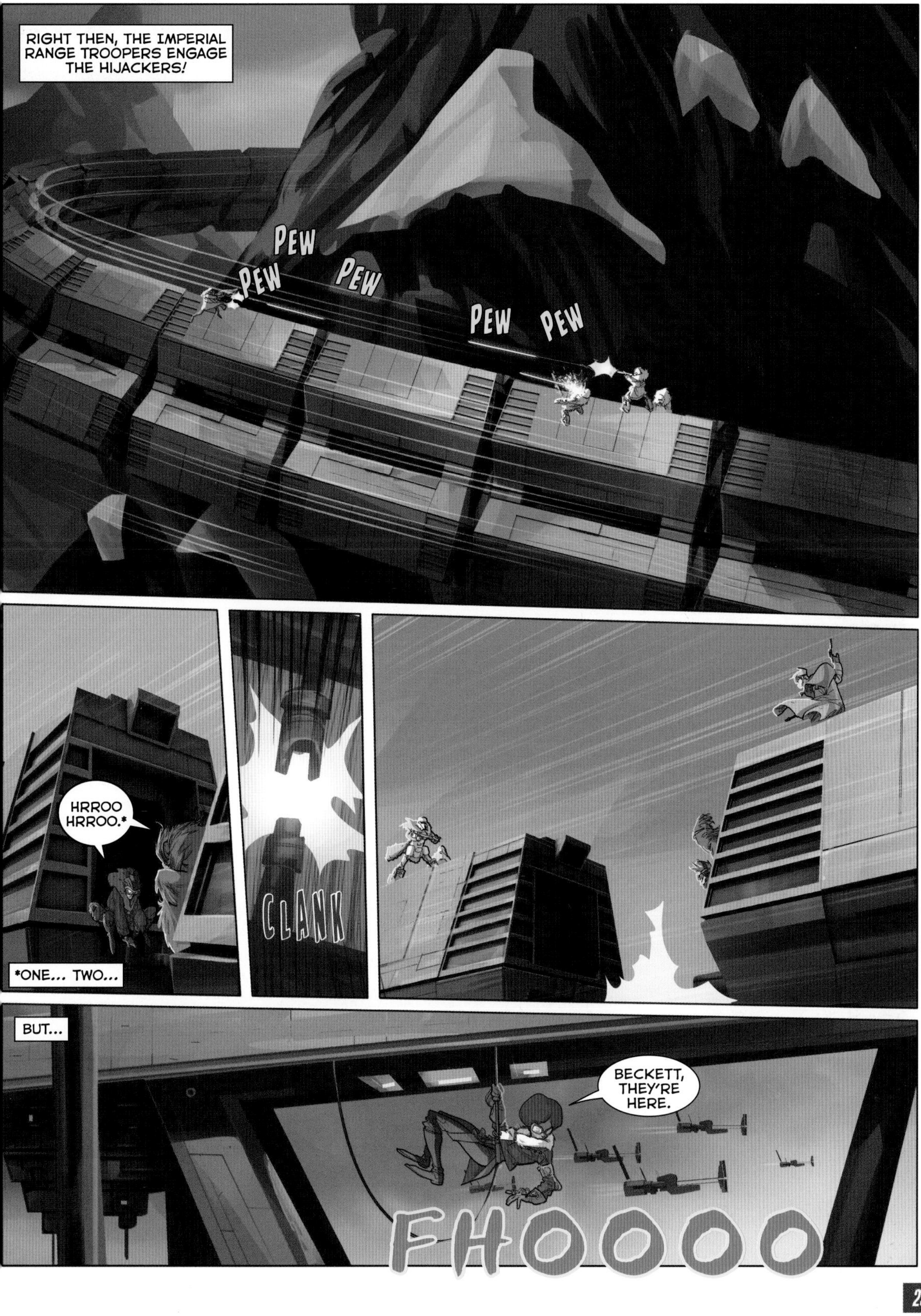
RIGHT THEN, THE IMPERIAL RANGE TROOPERS ENGAGE THE HIJACKERS!
PEW
PEW
PEW
PEW
PEW
HRROO HRROO.*
*ONE... TWO...
CLANK
BUT...
BECKETT, THEY'RE HERE.
FHOOOO

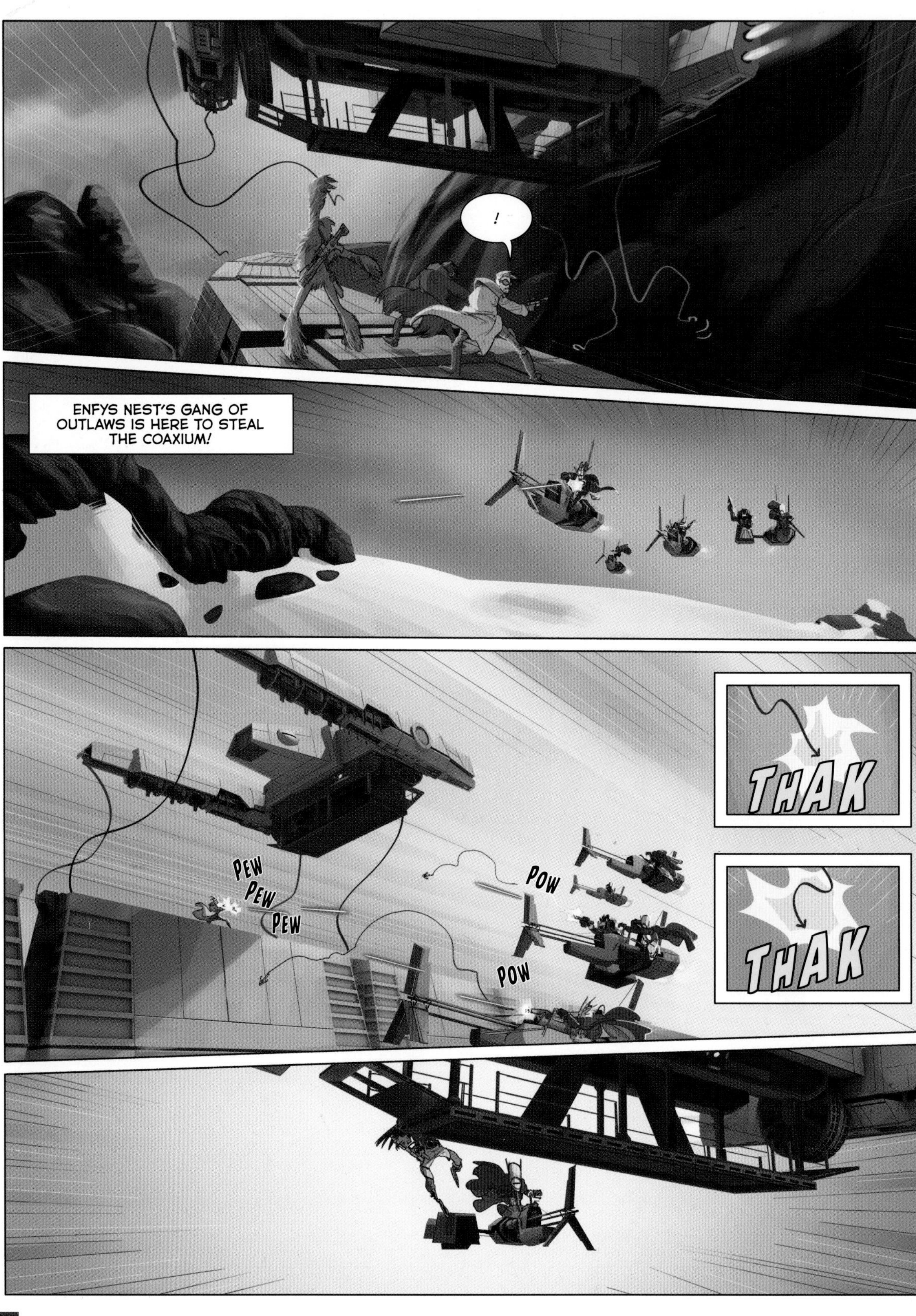
!
ENFYS NEST'S GANG OF OUTLAWS IS HERE TO STEAL THE COAXIUM!
PEW
PEW
PEW
POW
POW
THAK
THAK

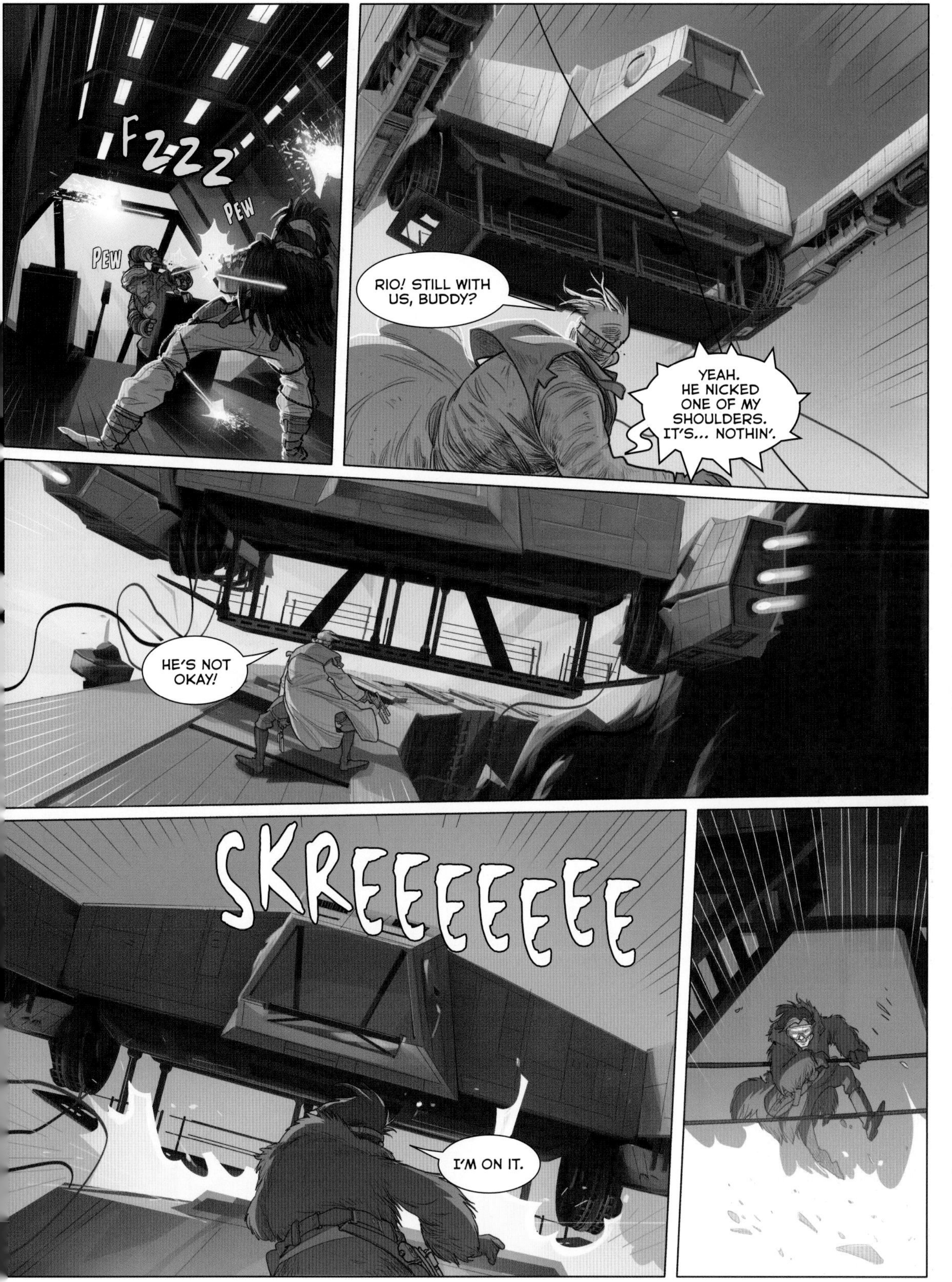

FZZZ
PEW
PEW
RIO! STILL WITH US, BUDDY?
YEAH. HE NICKED ONE OF MY SHOULDERS. IT'S... NOTHIN'.
HE'S NOT OKAY!
SKREEEEEEEE
I'M ON IT.

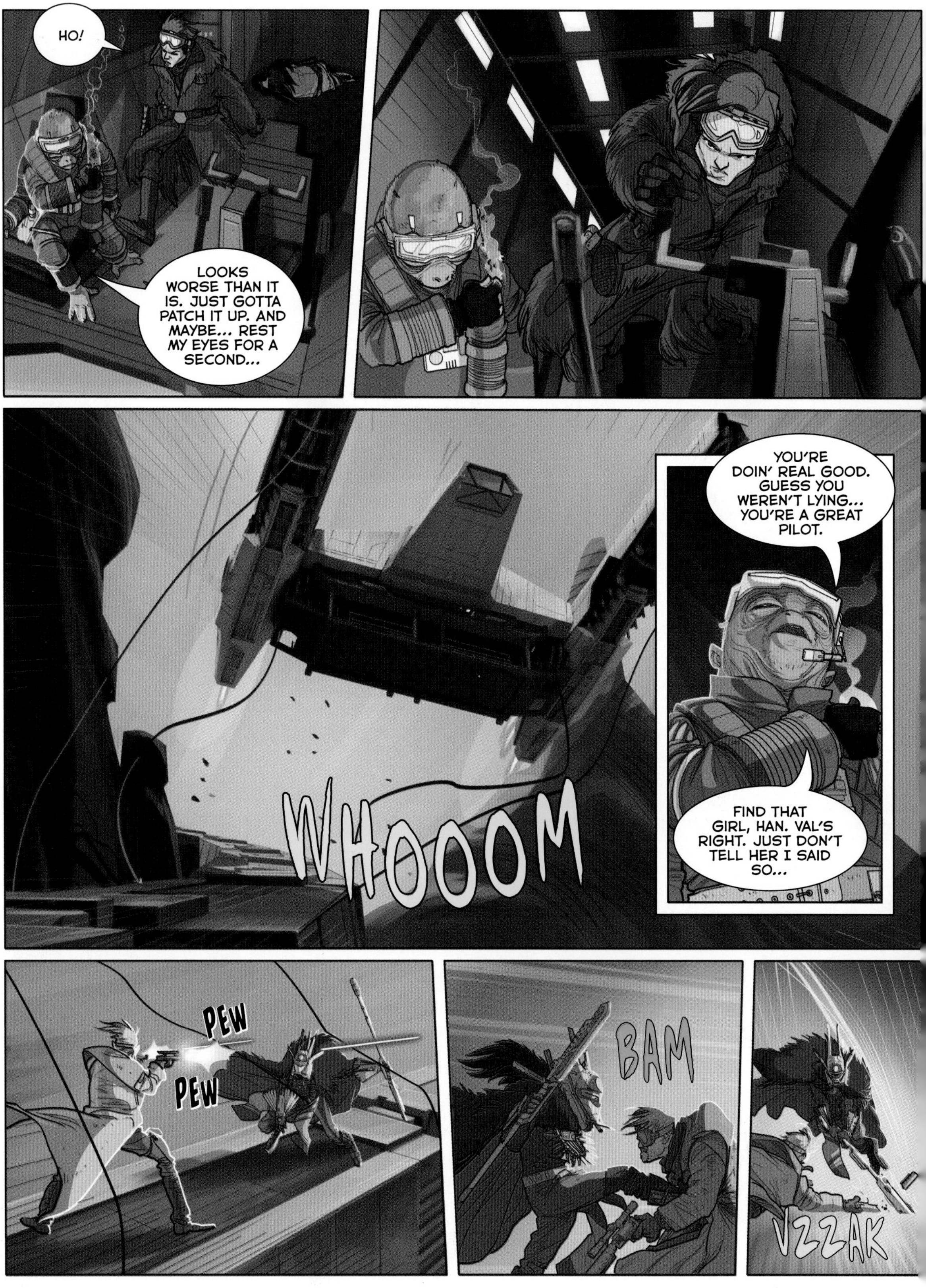
HO!
LOOKS WORSE THAN IT IS. JUST GOTTA PATCH IT UP. AND MAYBE... REST MY EYES FOR A SECOND...
WHOOOM
YOU'RE DOIN' REAL GOOD. GUESS YOU WEREN'T LYING... YOU'RE A GREAT PILOT.
FIND THAT GIRL, HAN. VAL'S RIGHT. JUST DON'T TELL HER I SAID SO...
PEW
PEW
BAM
VZZAK

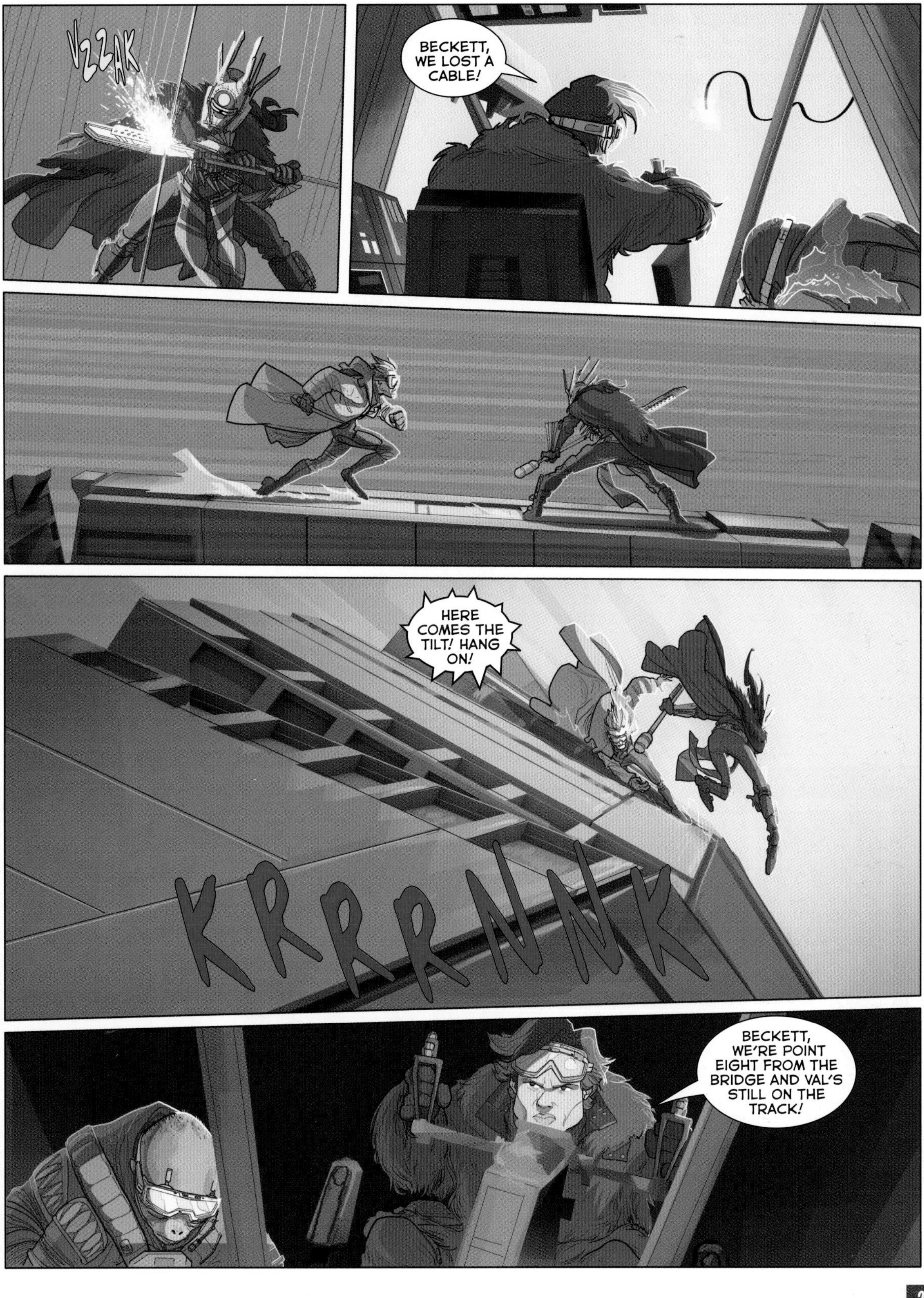
VZZAK
BECKETT, WE LOST A CABLE!
HERE COMES THE TILT! HANG ON!
KRRRNNK
BECKETT, WE'RE POINT EIGHT FROM THE BRIDGE AND VAL'S STILL ON THE TRACK!

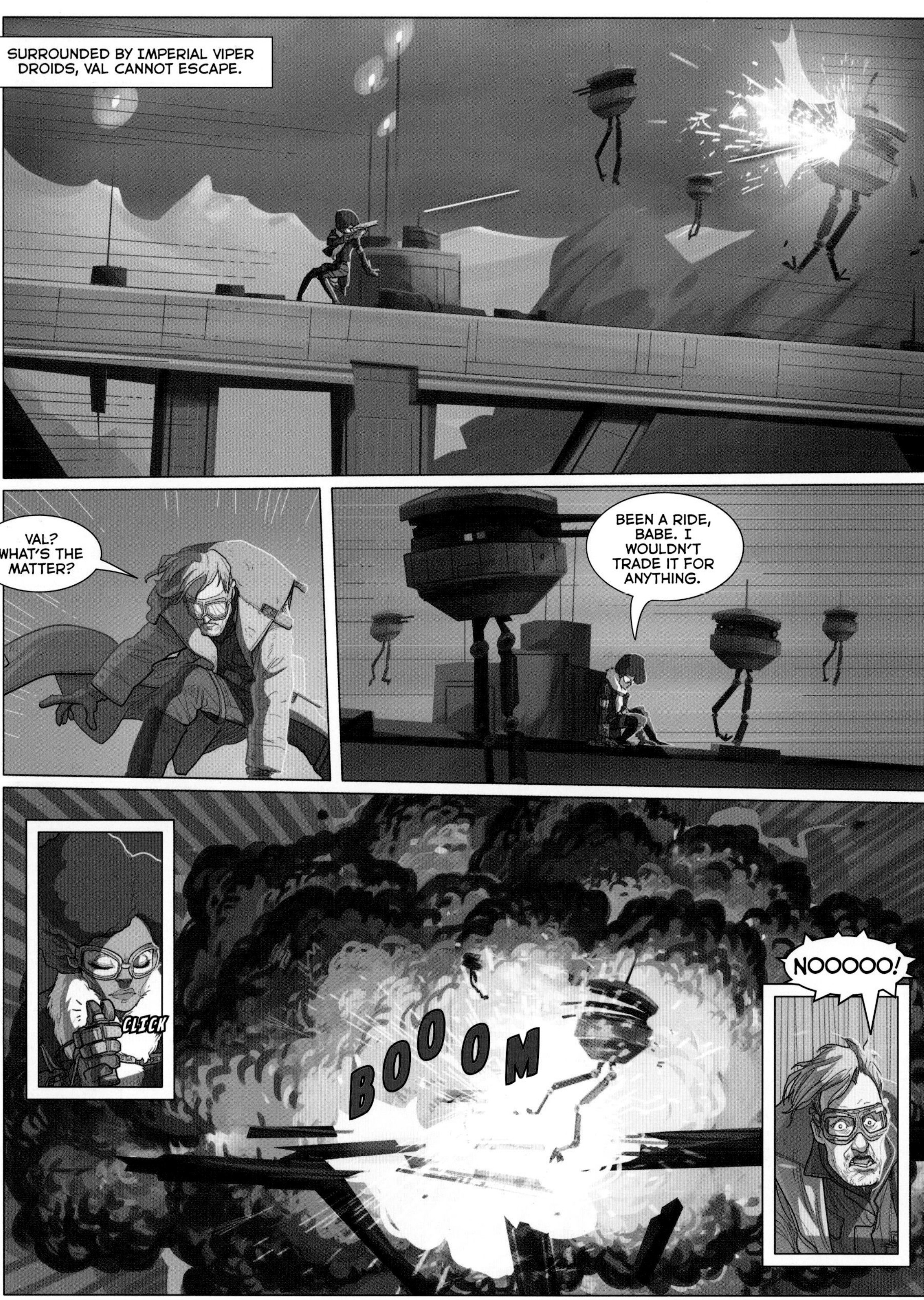
SURROUNDED BY IMPERIAL VIPER DROIDS, VAL CANNOT ESCAPE.
VAL? WHAT'S THE MATTER?
BEEN A RIDE, BABE. I WOULDN'T TRADE IT FOR ANYTHING.
CLICK
BOOOM
NOOOOO!

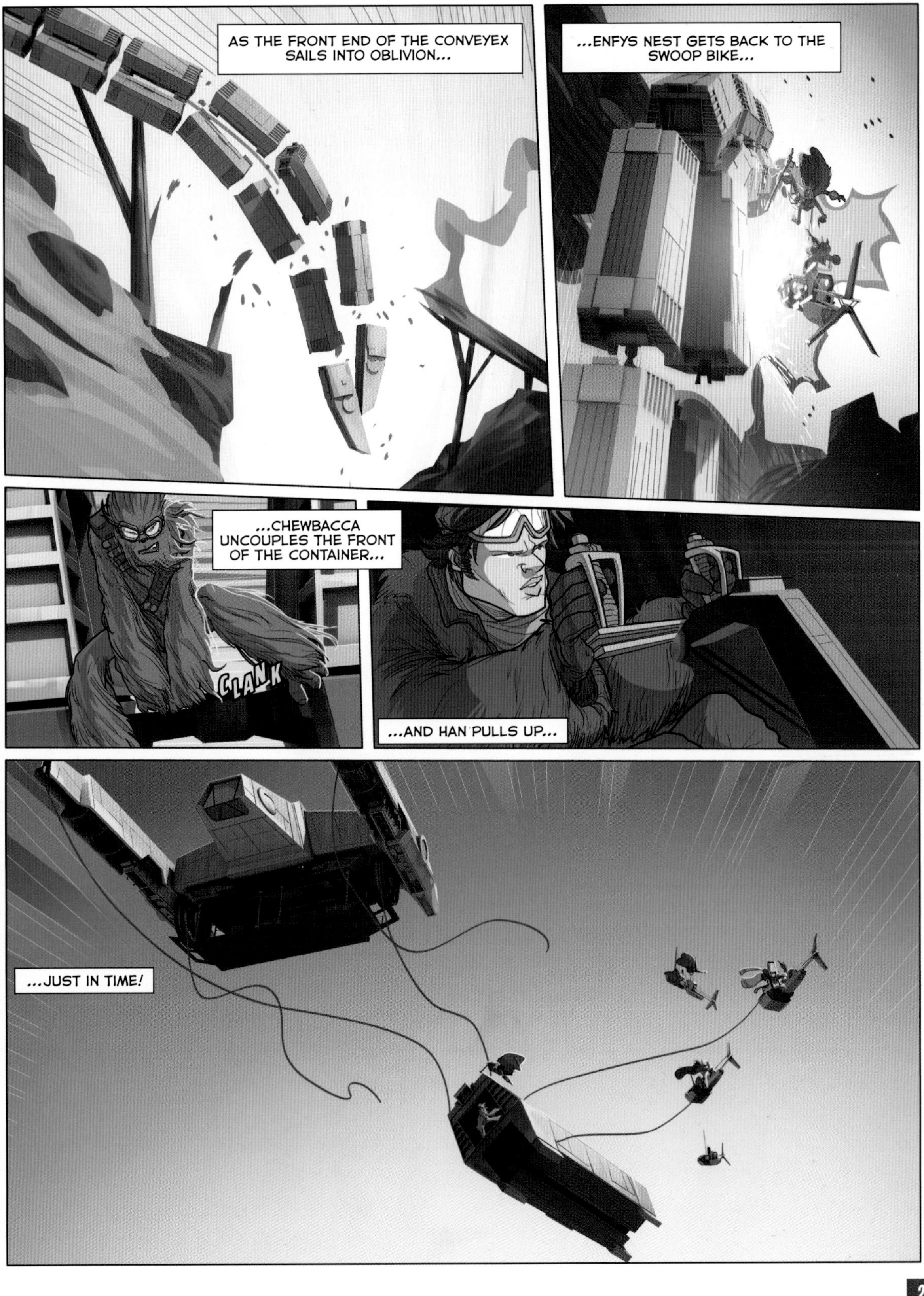
AS THE FRONT END OF THE CONVEYEX SAILS INTO OBLIVION...
...ENFYS NEST GETS BACK TO THE SWOOP BIKE...
...CHEWBACCA UNCOUPLES THE FRONT OF THE CONTAINER...
CLANK
...AND HAN PULLS UP...
...JUST IN TIME!

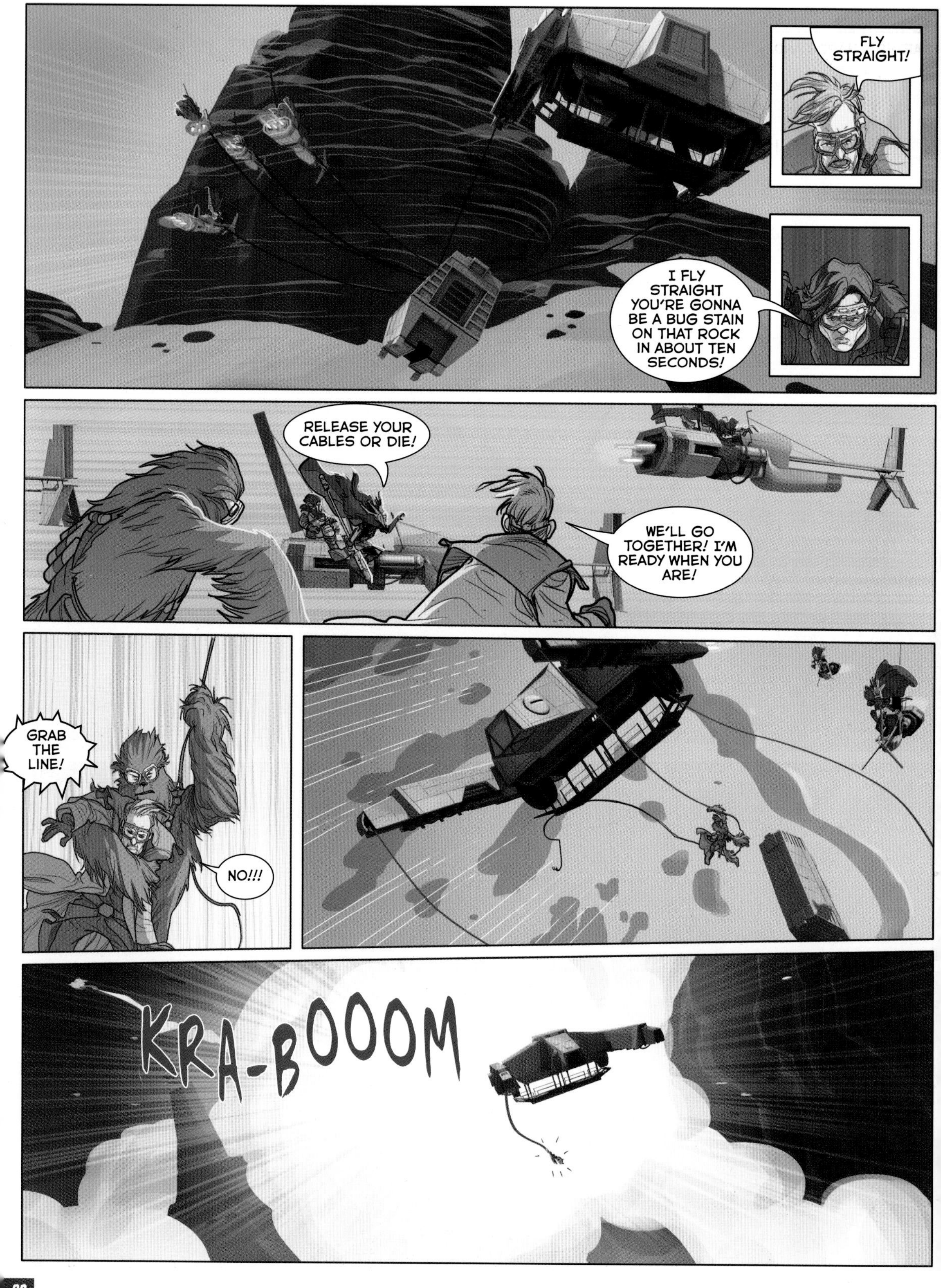
FLY STRAIGHT!
I FLY STRAIGHT YOU'RE GONNA BE A BUG STAIN ON THAT ROCK IN ABOUT TEN SECONDS!
RELEASE YOUR CABLES OR DIE!
WE'LL GO TOGETHER! I'M READY WHEN YOU ARE!
GRAB THE LINE!
NO!!!
KRA-BOOOM

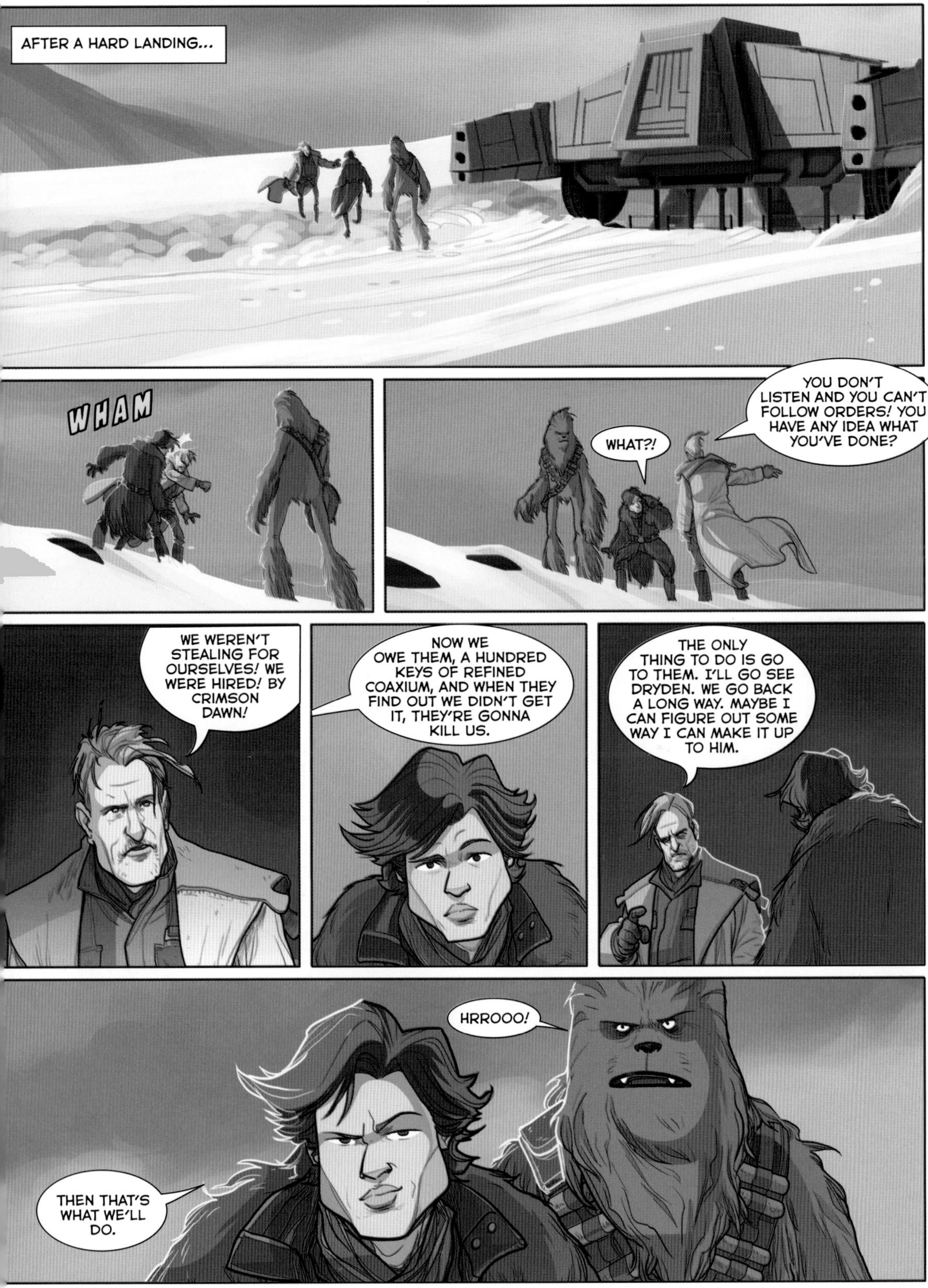
AFTER A HARD LANDING...
WHAM
WHAT?!
YOU DON'T LISTEN AND YOU CAN'T FOLLOW ORDERS! YOU HAVE ANY IDEA WHAT YOU'VE DONE?
WE WEREN'T STEALING FOR OURSELVES! WE WERE HIRED! BY CRIMSON DAWN!
NOW WE OWE THEM, A HUNDRED KEYS OF REFINED COAXIUM, AND WHEN THEY FIND OUT WE DIDN'T GET IT, THEY'RE GONNA KILL US.
THE ONLY THING TO DO IS GO TO THEM. I'LL GO SEE DRYDEN. WE GO BACK A LONG WAY. MAYBE I CAN FIGURE OUT SOME WAY I CAN MAKE IT UP TO HIM.
HRROOO!
THEN THAT'S WHAT WE'LL DO.

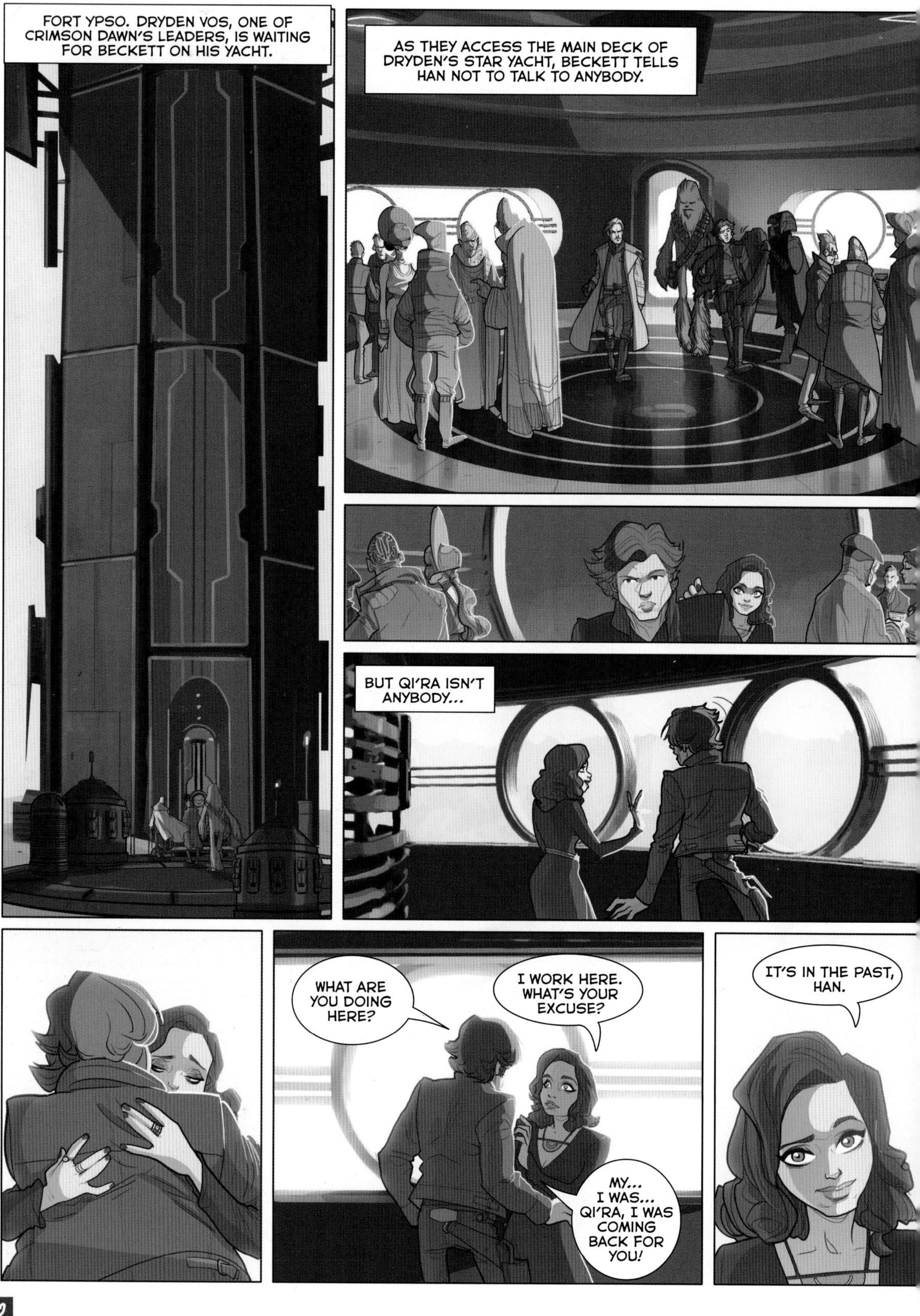
FORT YPSO. DRYDEN VOS, ONE OF CRIMSON DAWN'S LEADERS, IS WAITING FOR BECKETT ON HIS YACHT.
AS THEY ACCESS THE MAIN DECK OF DRYDEN'S STAR YACHT, BECKETT TELLS HAN NOT TO TALK TO ANYBODY.
BUT QI'RA ISN'T ANYBODY...
WHAT ARE YOU DOING HERE?
I WORK HERE. WHAT'S YOUR EXCUSE?
MY... I WAS... QI'RA, I WAS COMING BACK FOR YOU!
IT'S IN THE PAST, HAN.

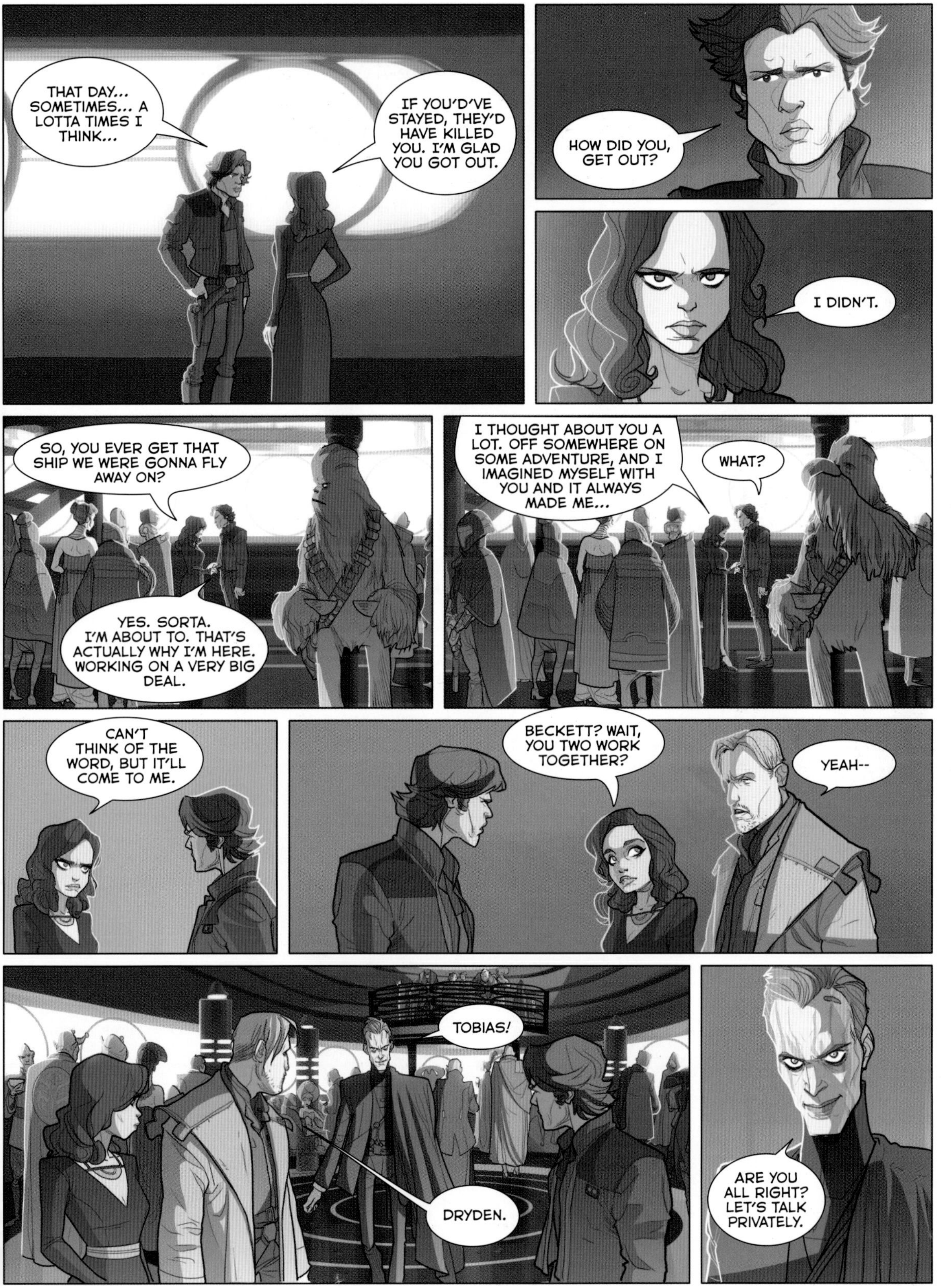

THAT DAY... SOMETIMES... A LOTTA TIMES I THINK...
IF YOU'D'VE STAYED, THEY'D HAVE KILLED YOU. I'M GLAD YOU GOT OUT.
HOW DID YOU, GET OUT?
I DIDN'T.
SO, YOU EVER GET THAT SHIP WE WERE GONNA FLY AWAY ON?
YES. SORTA. I'M ABOUT TO. THAT'S ACTUALLY WHY I'M HERE. WORKING ON A VERY BIG DEAL.
I THOUGHT ABOUT YOU A LOT. OFF SOMEWHERE ON SOME ADVENTURE, AND I IMAGINED MYSELF WITH YOU AND IT ALWAYS MADE ME...
WHAT?
CAN'T THINK OF THE WORD, BUT IT'LL COME TO ME.
BECKETT? WAIT, YOU TWO WORK TOGETHER?
YEAH--
TOBIAS!
DRYDEN.
ARE YOU ALL RIGHT? LET'S TALK PRIVATELY.

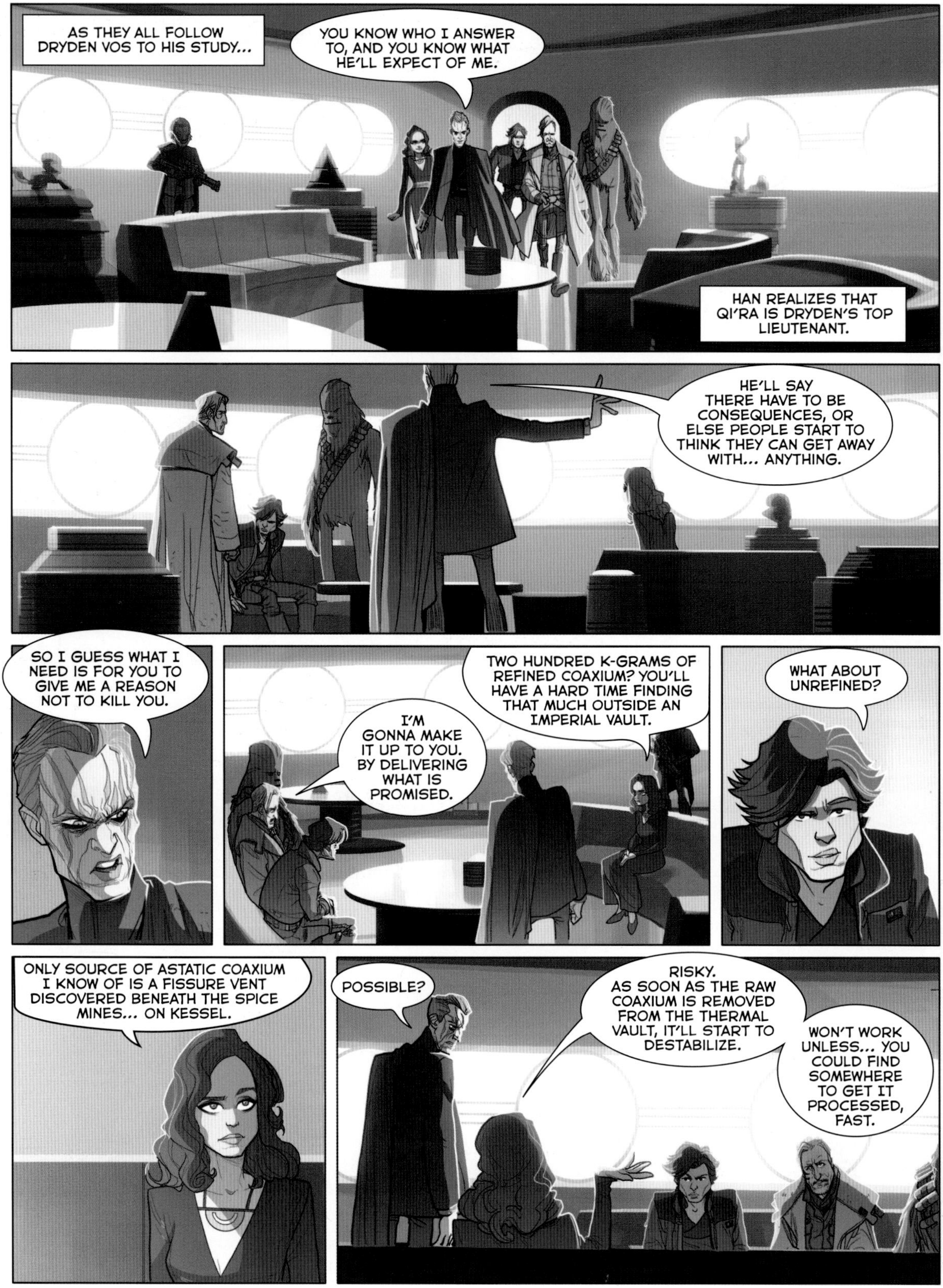
AS THEY ALL FOLLOW DRYDEN VOS TO HIS STUDY...
YOU KNOW WHO I ANSWER TO, AND YOU KNOW WHAT HE'LL EXPECT OF ME.
HAN REALIZES THAT QI'RA IS DRYDEN'S TOP LIEUTENANT.
HE'LL SAY THERE HAVE TO BE CONSEQUENCES, OR ELSE PEOPLE START TO THINK THEY CAN GET AWAY WITH... ANYTHING.
SO I GUESS WHAT I NEED IS FOR YOU TO GIVE ME A REASON NOT TO KILL YOU.
I'M GONNA MAKE IT UP TO YOU. BY DELIVERING WHAT IS PROMISED.
TWO HUNDRED K-GRAMS OF REFINED COAXIUM? YOU'LL HAVE A HARD TIME FINDING THAT MUCH OUTSIDE AN IMPERIAL VAULT.
WHAT ABOUT UNREFINED?
ONLY SOURCE OF ASTATIC COAXIUM I KNOW OF IS A FISSURE VENT DISCOVERED BENEATH THE SPICE MINES... ON KESSEL.
POSSIBLE?
RISKY. AS SOON AS THE RAW COAXIUM IS REMOVED FROM THE THERMAL VAULT, IT'LL START TO DESTABILIZE.
WON'T WORK UNLESS... YOU COULD FIND SOMEWHERE TO GET IT PROCESSED, FAST.

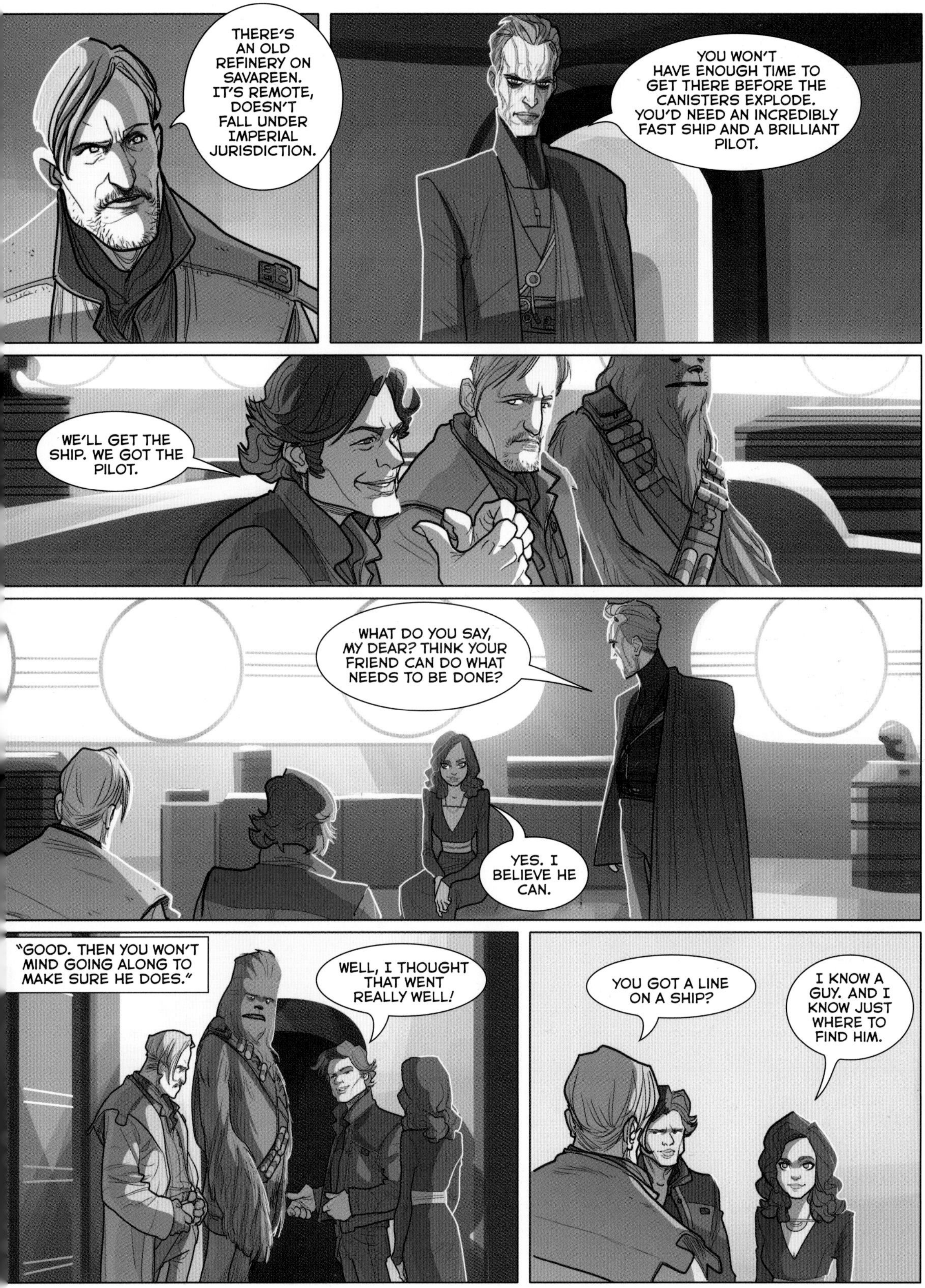
THERE'S AN OLD REFINERY ON SAVAREEN. IT'S REMOTE, DOESN'T FALL UNDER IMPERIAL JURISDICTION.
YOU WON'T HAVE ENOUGH TIME TO GET THERE BEFORE THE CANISTERS EXPLODE. YOU'D NEED AN INCREDIBLY FAST SHIP AND A BRILLIANT PILOT.
WE'LL GET THE SHIP. WE GOT THE PILOT.
WHAT DO YOU SAY, MY DEAR? THINK YOUR FRIEND CAN DO WHAT NEEDS TO BE DONE?
YES. I BELIEVE HE CAN.
"GOOD. THEN YOU WON'T MIND GOING ALONG TO MAKE SURE HE DOES."
WELL, I THOUGHT THAT WENT REALLY WELL!
YOU GOT A LINE ON A SHIP?
I KNOW A GUY. AND I KNOW JUST WHERE TO FIND HIM.

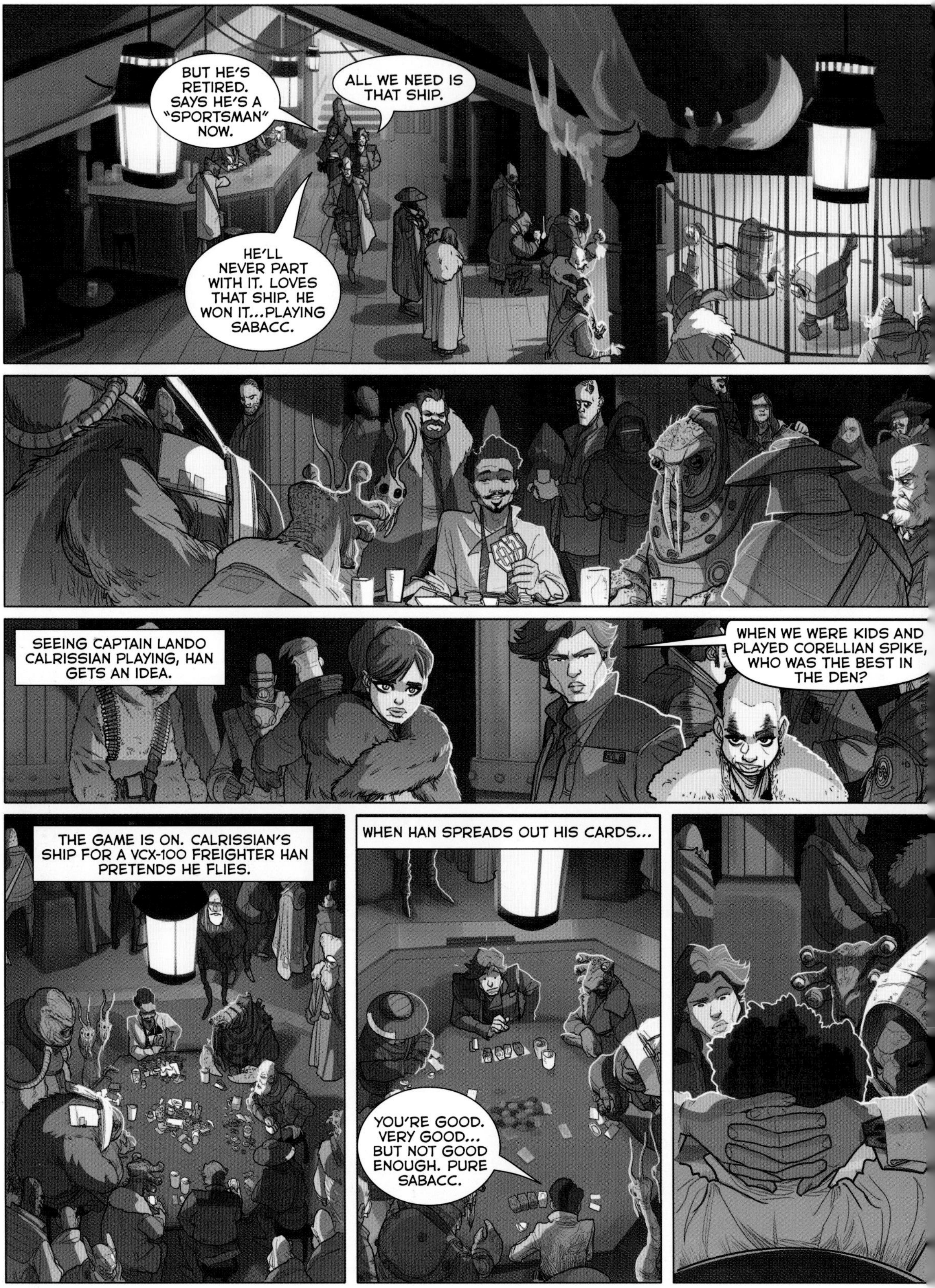

BUT HE'S RETIRED. SAYS HE'S A "SPORTSMAN" NOW.
ALL WE NEED IS THAT SHIP.
HE'LL NEVER PART WITH IT. LOVES THAT SHIP. HE WON IT...PLAYING SABACC.
SEEING CAPTAIN LANDO CALRISSIAN PLAYING, HAN GETS AN IDEA.
WHEN WE WERE KIDS AND PLAYED CORELLIAN SPIKE, WHO WAS THE BEST IN THE DEN?
THE GAME IS ON. CALRISSIAN'S SHIP FOR A VCX-100 FREIGHTER HAN PRETENDS HE FLIES.
WHEN HAN SPREADS OUT HIS CARDS...
YOU'RE GOOD. VERY GOOD... BUT NOT GOOD ENOUGH. PURE SABACC.

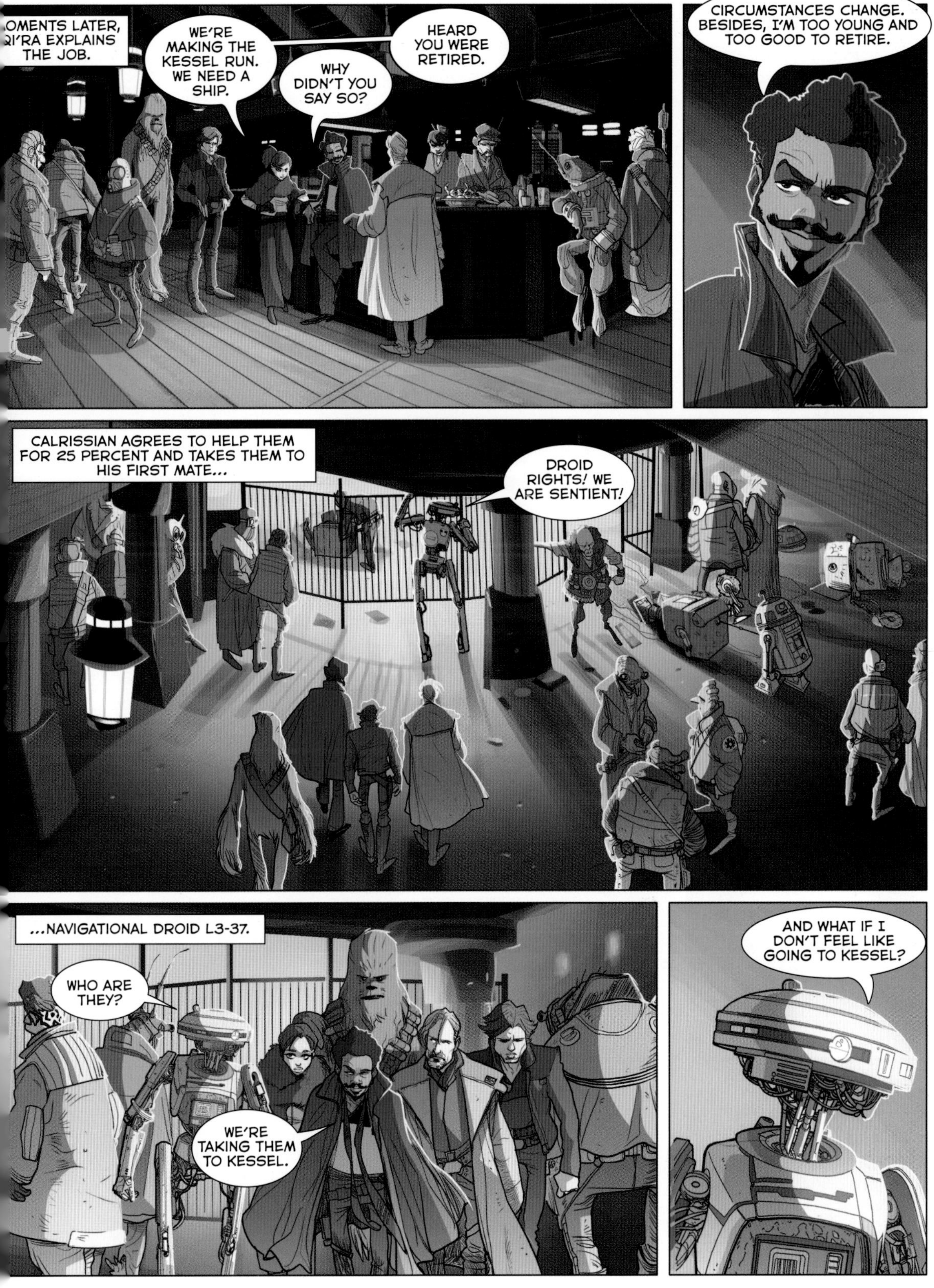
OMENTS LATER, QI'RA EXPLAINS THE JOB.
WE'RE MAKING THE KESSEL RUN. WE NEED A SHIP.
HEARD YOU WERE RETIRED.
WHY DIDN'T YOU SAY SO?
CIRCUMSTANCES CHANGE. BESIDES, I'M TOO YOUNG AND TOO GOOD TO RETIRE.
CALRISSIAN AGREES TO HELP THEM FOR 25 PERCENT AND TAKES THEM TO HIS FIRST MATE...
DROID RIGHTS! WE ARE SENTIENT!
...NAVIGATIONAL DROID L3-37.
WHO ARE THEY?
WE'RE TAKING THEM TO KESSEL.
AND WHAT IF I DON'T FEEL LIKE GOING TO KESSEL?

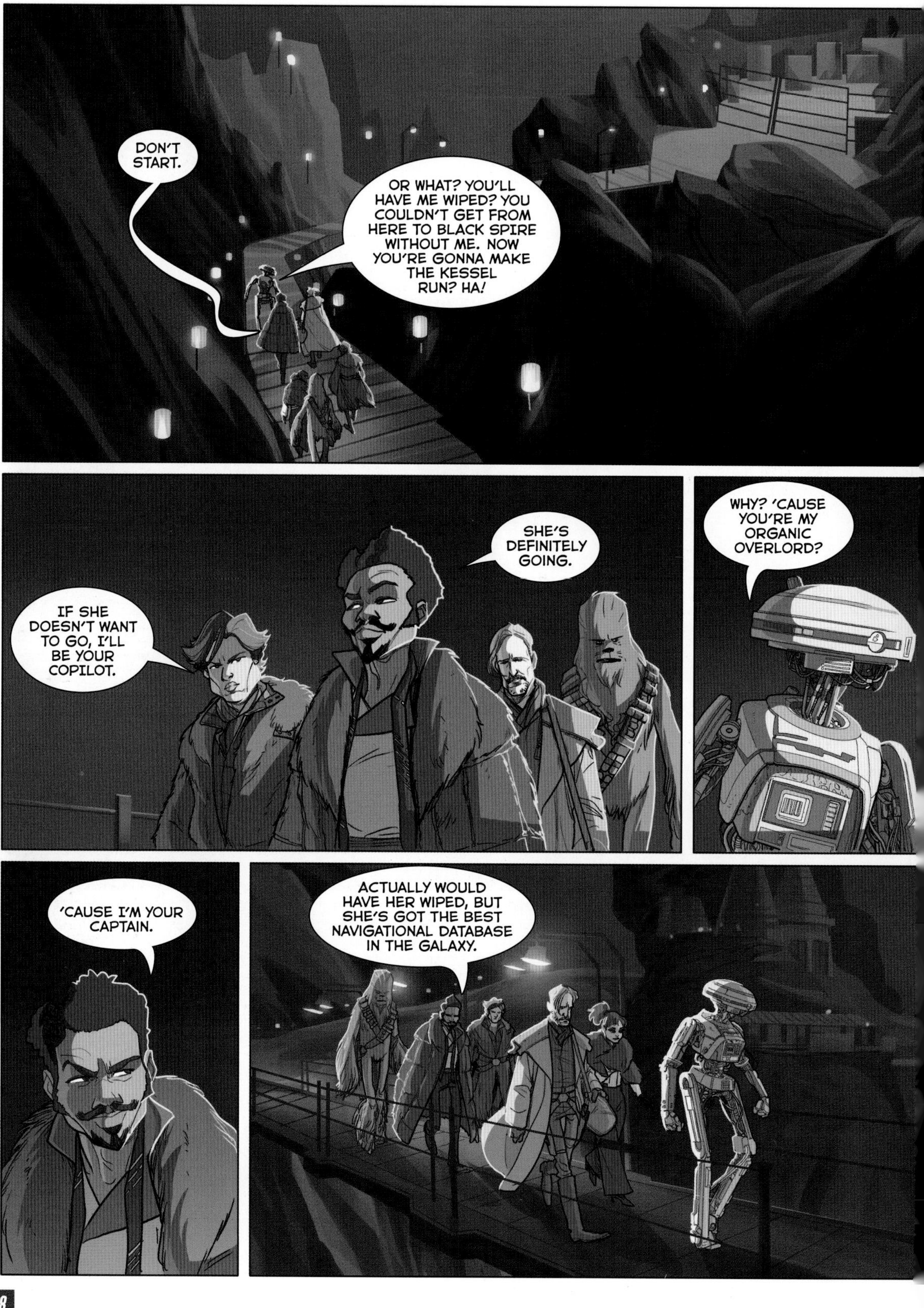
DON'T START.
OR WHAT? YOU'LL HAVE ME WIPED? YOU COULDN'T GET FROM HERE TO BLACK SPIRE WITHOUT ME. NOW YOU'RE GONNA MAKE THE KESSEL RUN? HA!
SHE'S DEFINITELY GOING.
IF SHE DOESN'T WANT TO GO, I'LL BE YOUR COPILOT.
WHY? 'CAUSE YOU'RE MY ORGANIC OVERLORD?
'CAUSE I'M YOUR CAPTAIN.
ACTUALLY WOULD HAVE HER WIPED, BUT SHE'S GOT THE BEST NAVIGATIONAL DATABASE IN THE GALAXY.

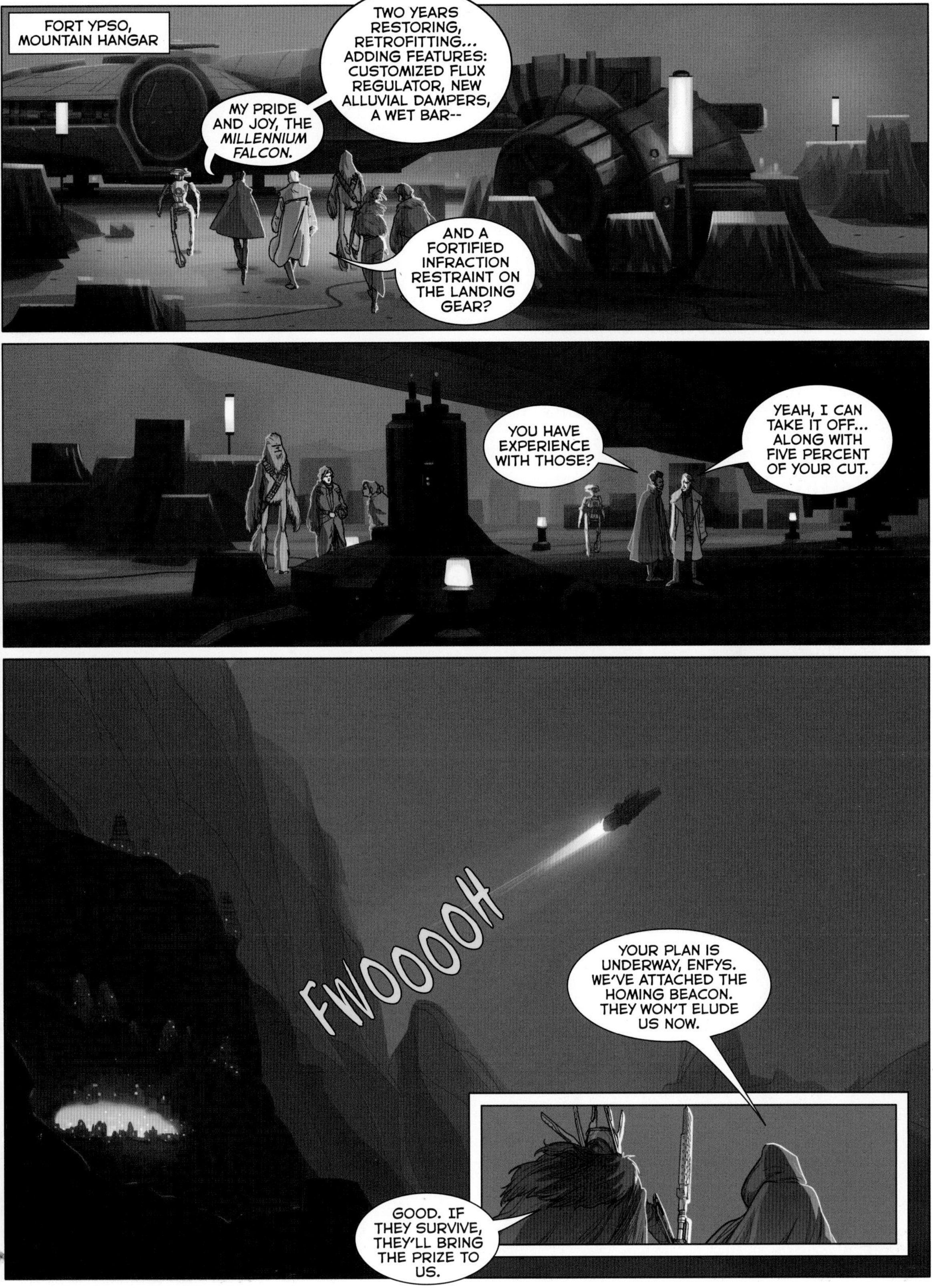
FORT YPSO, MOUNTAIN HANGAR
MY PRIDE AND JOY, THE *MILLENNIUM FALCON.*
TWO YEARS RESTORING, RETROFITTING... ADDING FEATURES: CUSTOMIZED FLUX REGULATOR, NEW ALLUVIAL DAMPERS, A WET BAR--
AND A FORTIFIED INFRACTION RESTRAINT ON THE LANDING GEAR?
YOU HAVE EXPERIENCE WITH THOSE?
YEAH, I CAN TAKE IT OFF... ALONG WITH FIVE PERCENT OF YOUR CUT.
FWOOOOH
YOUR PLAN IS UNDERWAY, ENFYS. WE'VE ATTACHED THE HOMING BEACON. THEY WON'T ELUDE US NOW.
GOOD. IF THEY SURVIVE, THEY'LL BRING THE PRIZE TO US.

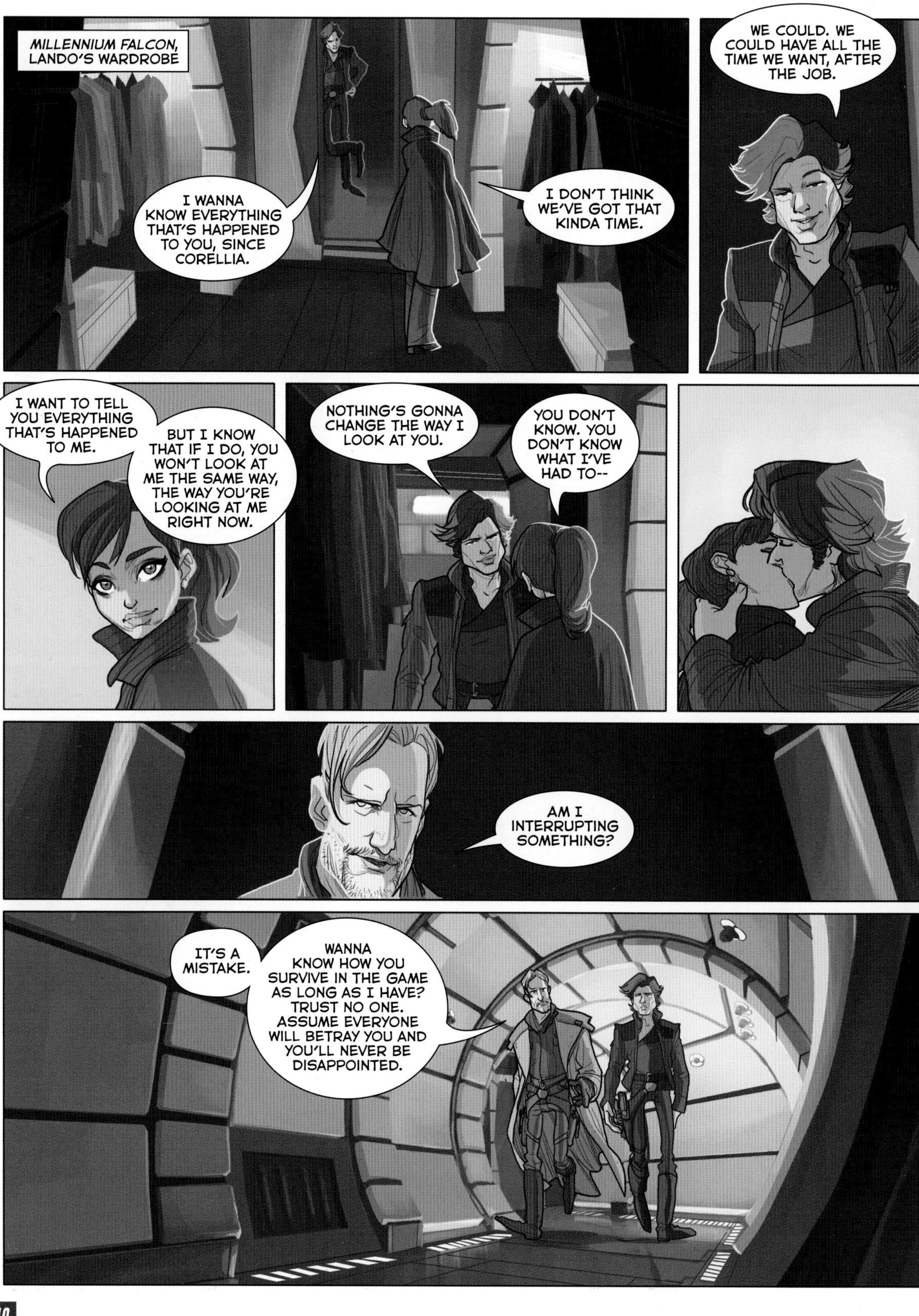
MILLENNIUM FALCON, LANDO'S WARDROBE
I WANNA KNOW EVERYTHING THAT'S HAPPENED TO YOU, SINCE CORELLIA.
I DON'T THINK WE'VE GOT THAT KINDA TIME.
WE COULD. WE COULD HAVE ALL THE TIME WE WANT, AFTER THE JOB.
I WANT TO TELL YOU EVERYTHING THAT'S HAPPENED TO ME.
BUT I KNOW THAT IF I DO, YOU WON'T LOOK AT ME THE SAME WAY, THE WAY YOU'RE LOOKING AT ME RIGHT NOW.
NOTHING'S GONNA CHANGE THE WAY I LOOK AT YOU.
YOU DON'T KNOW. YOU DON'T KNOW WHAT I'VE HAD TO--
AM I INTERRUPTING SOMETHING?
IT'S A MISTAKE.
WANNA KNOW HOW YOU SURVIVE IN THE GAME AS LONG AS I HAVE? TRUST NO ONE. ASSUME EVERYONE WILL BETRAY YOU AND YOU'LL NEVER BE DISAPPOINTED.

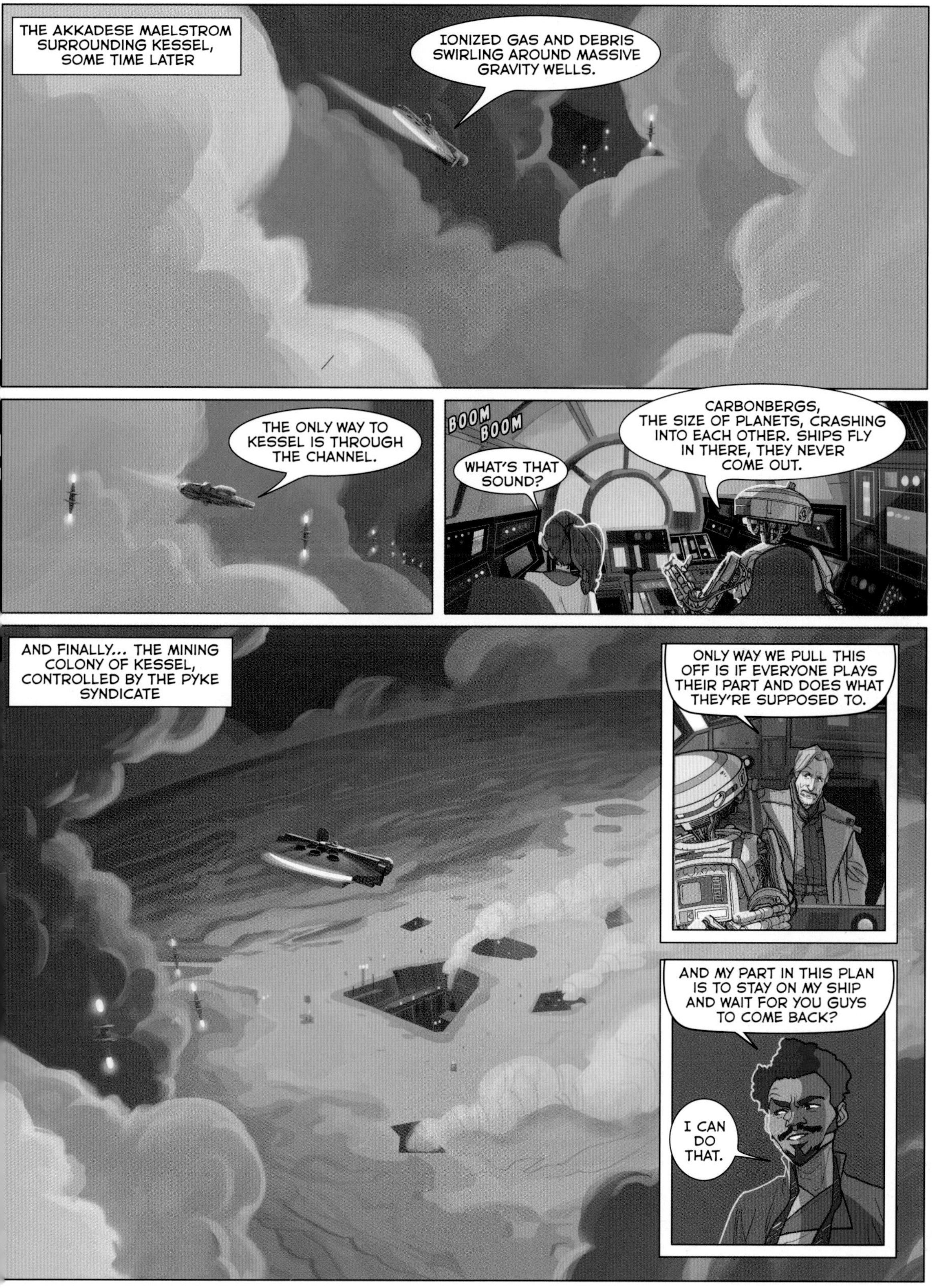
THE AKKADESE MAELSTROM SURROUNDING KESSEL, SOME TIME LATER
IONIZED GAS AND DEBRIS SWIRLING AROUND MASSIVE GRAVITY WELLS.
THE ONLY WAY TO KESSEL IS THROUGH THE CHANNEL.
BOOM BOOM
WHAT'S THAT SOUND?
CARBONBERGS, THE SIZE OF PLANETS, CRASHING INTO EACH OTHER. SHIPS FLY IN THERE, THEY NEVER COME OUT.
AND FINALLY... THE MINING COLONY OF KESSEL, CONTROLLED BY THE PYKE SYNDICATE
ONLY WAY WE PULL THIS OFF IS IF EVERYONE PLAYS THEIR PART AND DOES WHAT THEY'RE SUPPOSED TO.
AND MY PART IN THIS PLAN IS TO STAY ON MY SHIP AND WAIT FOR YOU GUYS TO COME BACK?
I CAN DO THAT.

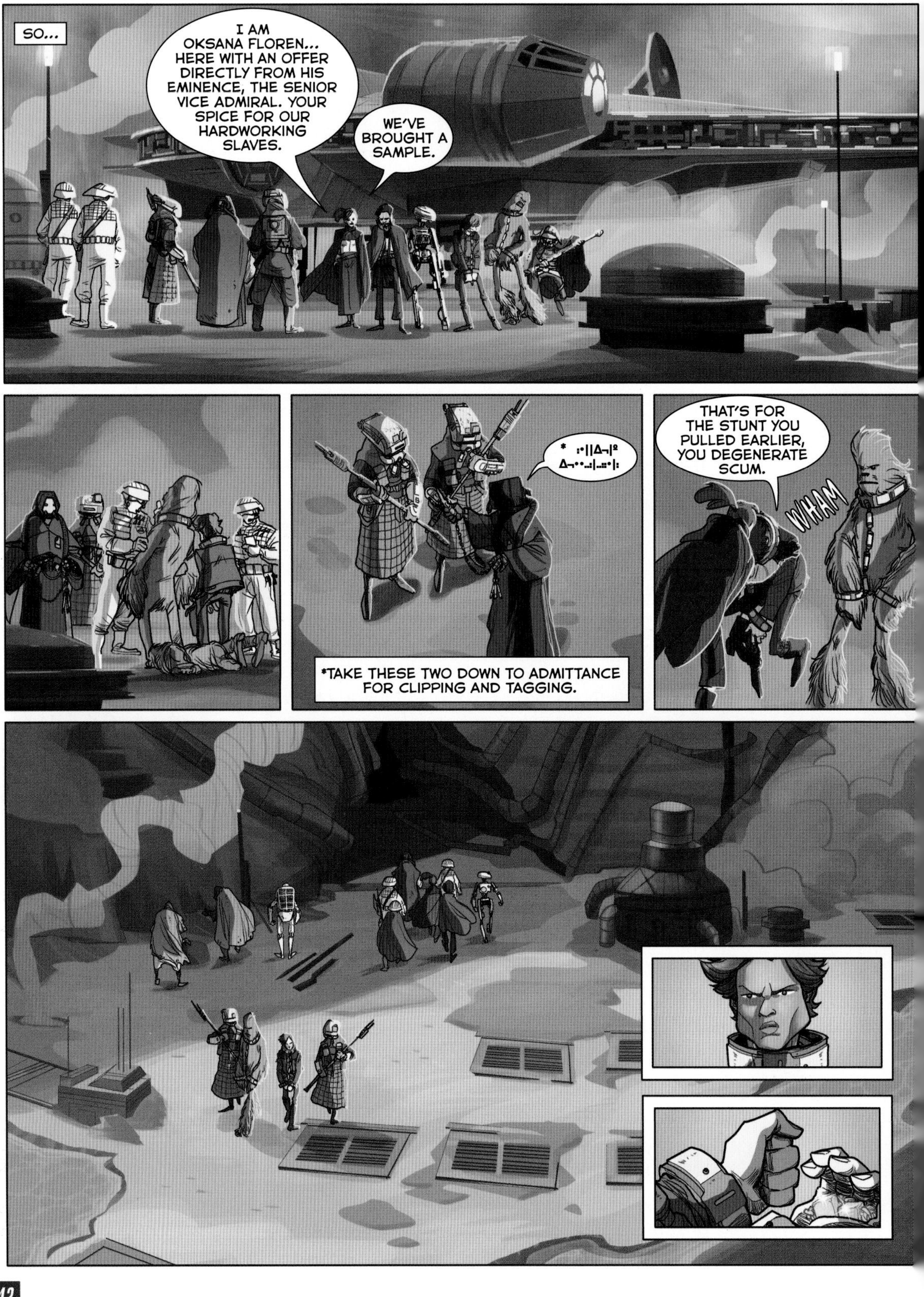
SO...
I AM OKSANA FLOREN... HERE WITH AN OFFER DIRECTLY FROM HIS EMINENCE, THE SENIOR VICE ADMIRAL. YOUR SPICE FOR OUR HARDWORKING SLAVES.
WE'VE BROUGHT A SAMPLE.
*TAKE THESE TWO DOWN TO ADMITTANCE FOR CLIPPING AND TAGGING.
THAT'S FOR THE STUNT YOU PULLED EARLIER, YOU DEGENERATE SCUM.
WHAM

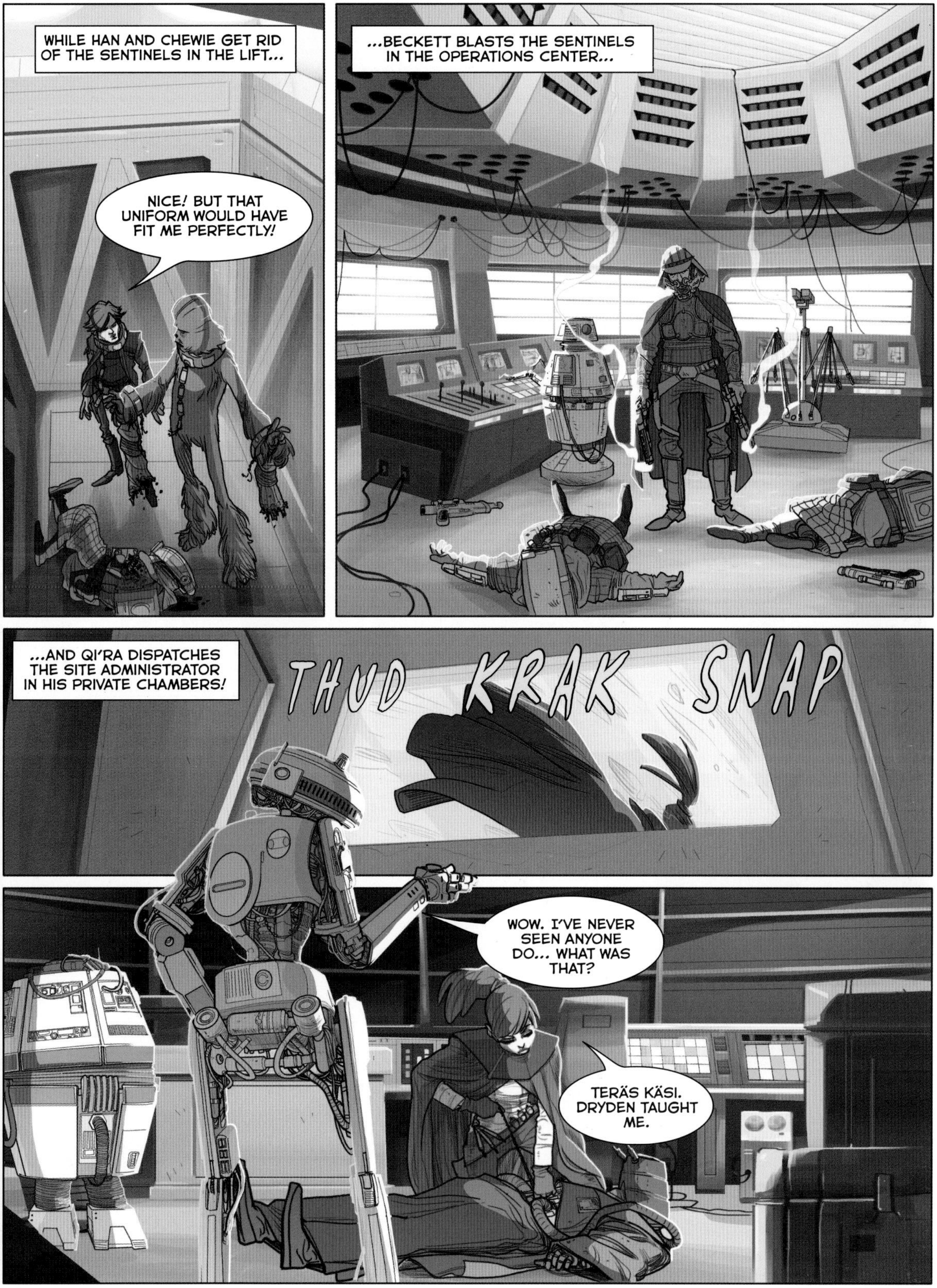

WHILE HAN AND CHEWIE GET RID OF THE SENTINELS IN THE LIFT...
NICE! BUT THAT UNIFORM WOULD HAVE FIT ME PERFECTLY!
...BECKETT BLASTS THE SENTINELS IN THE OPERATIONS CENTER...
...AND QI'RA DISPATCHES THE SITE ADMINISTRATOR IN HIS PRIVATE CHAMBERS!
THUD KRAK SNAP
WOW. I'VE NEVER SEEN ANYONE DO... WHAT WAS THAT?
TERÄS KÄSI. DRYDEN TAUGHT ME.

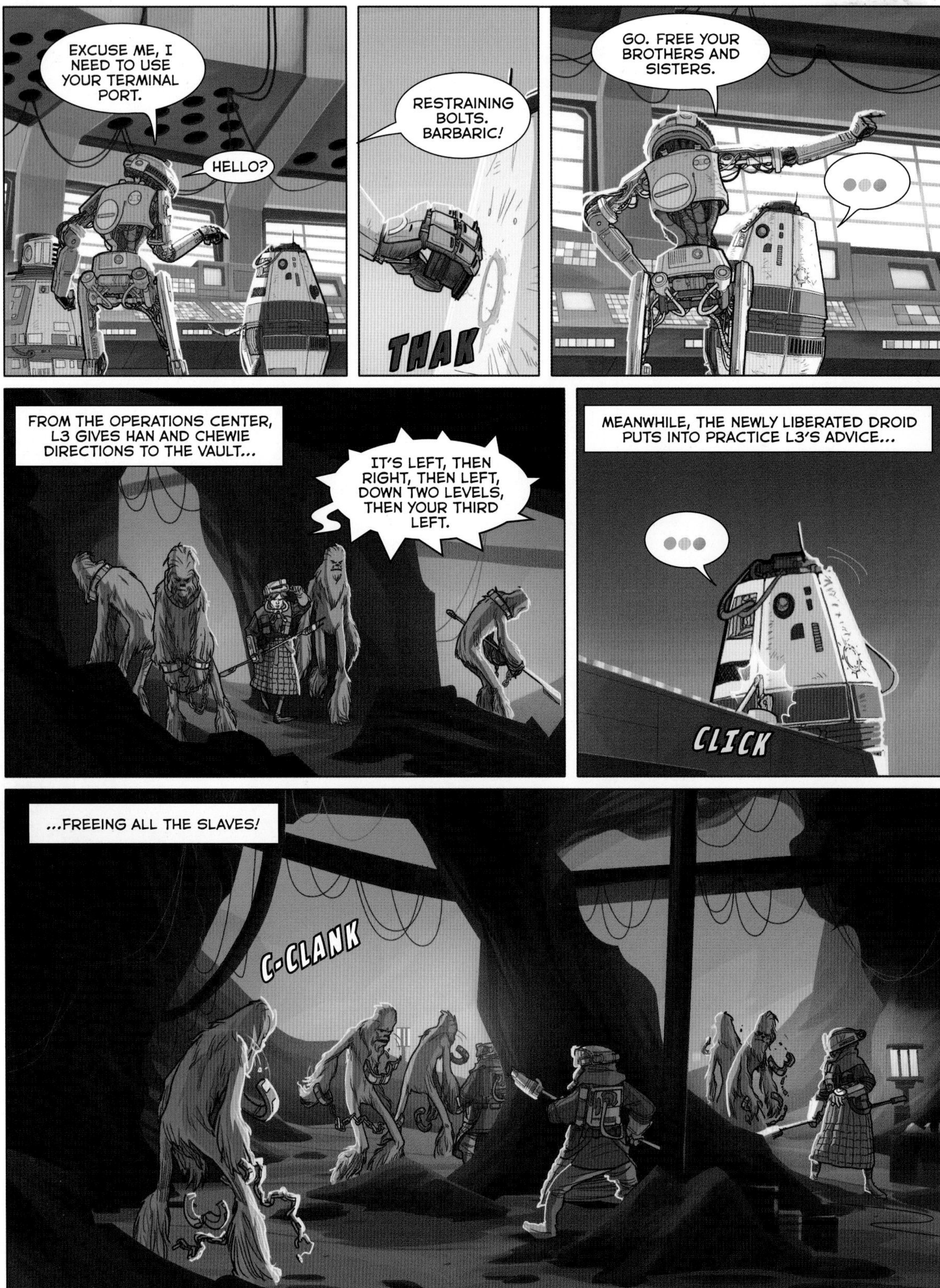
EXCUSE ME, I NEED TO USE YOUR TERMINAL PORT.
HELLO?
RESTRAINING BOLTS. BARBARIC!
THAK
GO. FREE YOUR BROTHERS AND SISTERS.
FROM THE OPERATIONS CENTER, L3 GIVES HAN AND CHEWIE DIRECTIONS TO THE VAULT...
IT'S LEFT, THEN RIGHT, THEN LEFT, DOWN TWO LEVELS, THEN YOUR THIRD LEFT.
MEANWHILE, THE NEWLY LIBERATED DROID PUTS INTO PRACTICE L3'S ADVICE...
CLICK
...FREEING ALL THE SLAVES!
C-CLANK

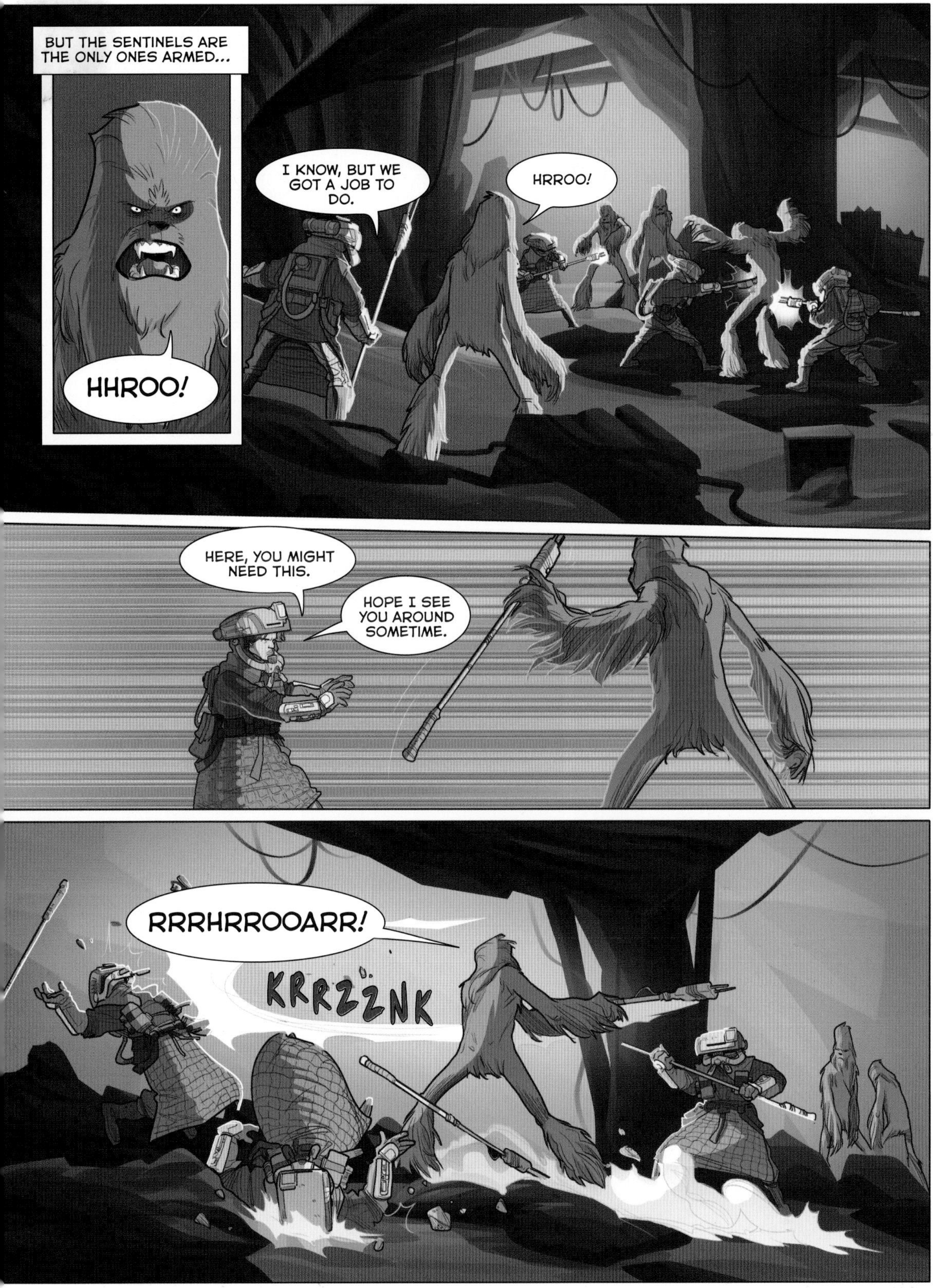
BUT THE SENTINELS ARE THE ONLY ONES ARMED...
HHROO!
I KNOW, BUT WE GOT A JOB TO DO.
HRROO!
HERE, YOU MIGHT NEED THIS.
HOPE I SEE YOU AROUND SOMETIME.
RRRHRROOARR!
KRRZZNK

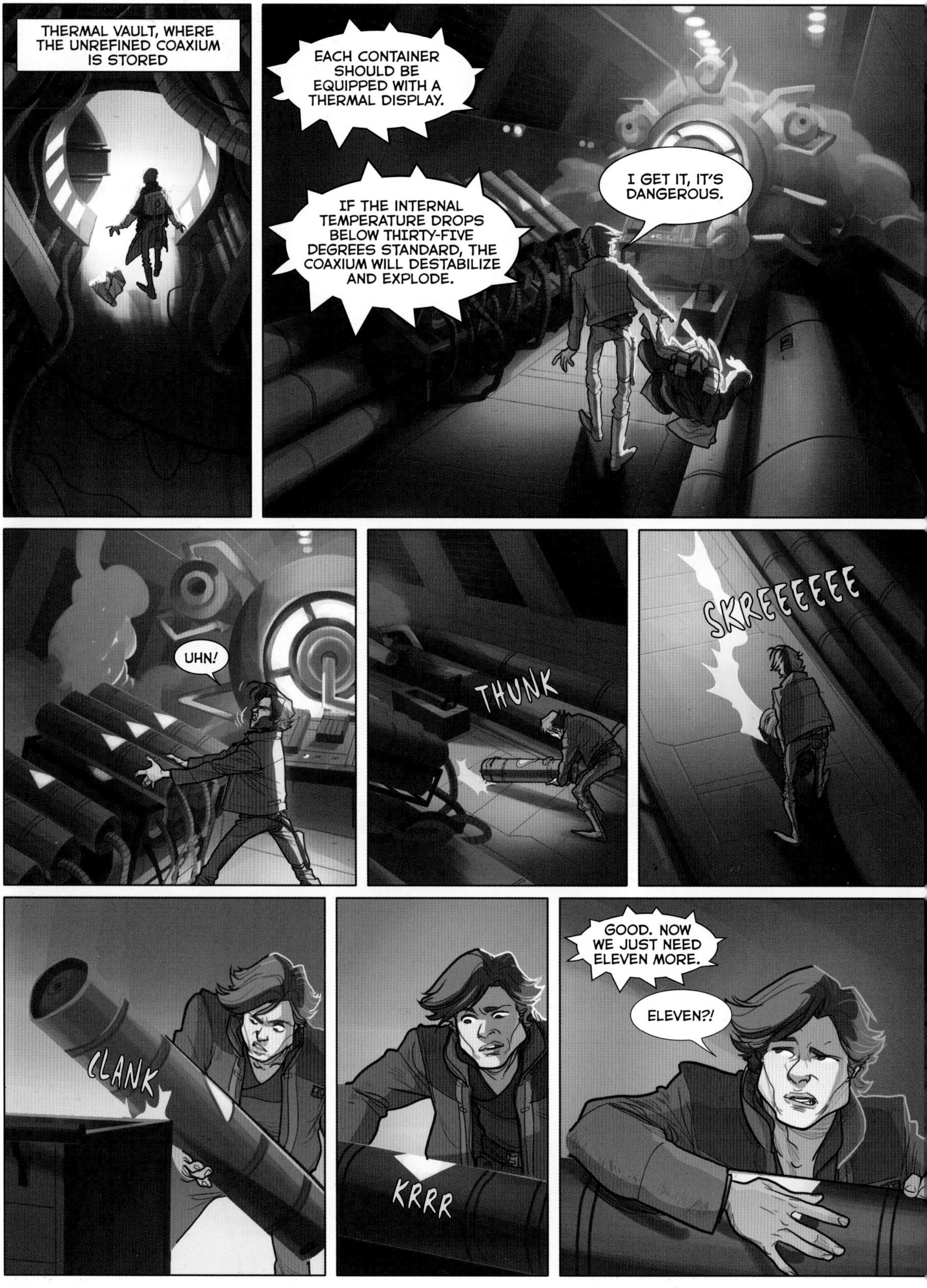
THERMAL VAULT, WHERE THE UNREFINED COAXIUM IS STORED
EACH CONTAINER SHOULD BE EQUIPPED WITH A THERMAL DISPLAY.
IF THE INTERNAL TEMPERATURE DROPS BELOW THIRTY-FIVE DEGREES STANDARD, THE COAXIUM WILL DESTABILIZE AND EXPLODE.
I GET IT, IT'S DANGEROUS.
UHN!
THUNK
SKREEEEEEE
CLANK
KRRR
GOOD. NOW WE JUST NEED ELEVEN MORE.
ELEVEN?!

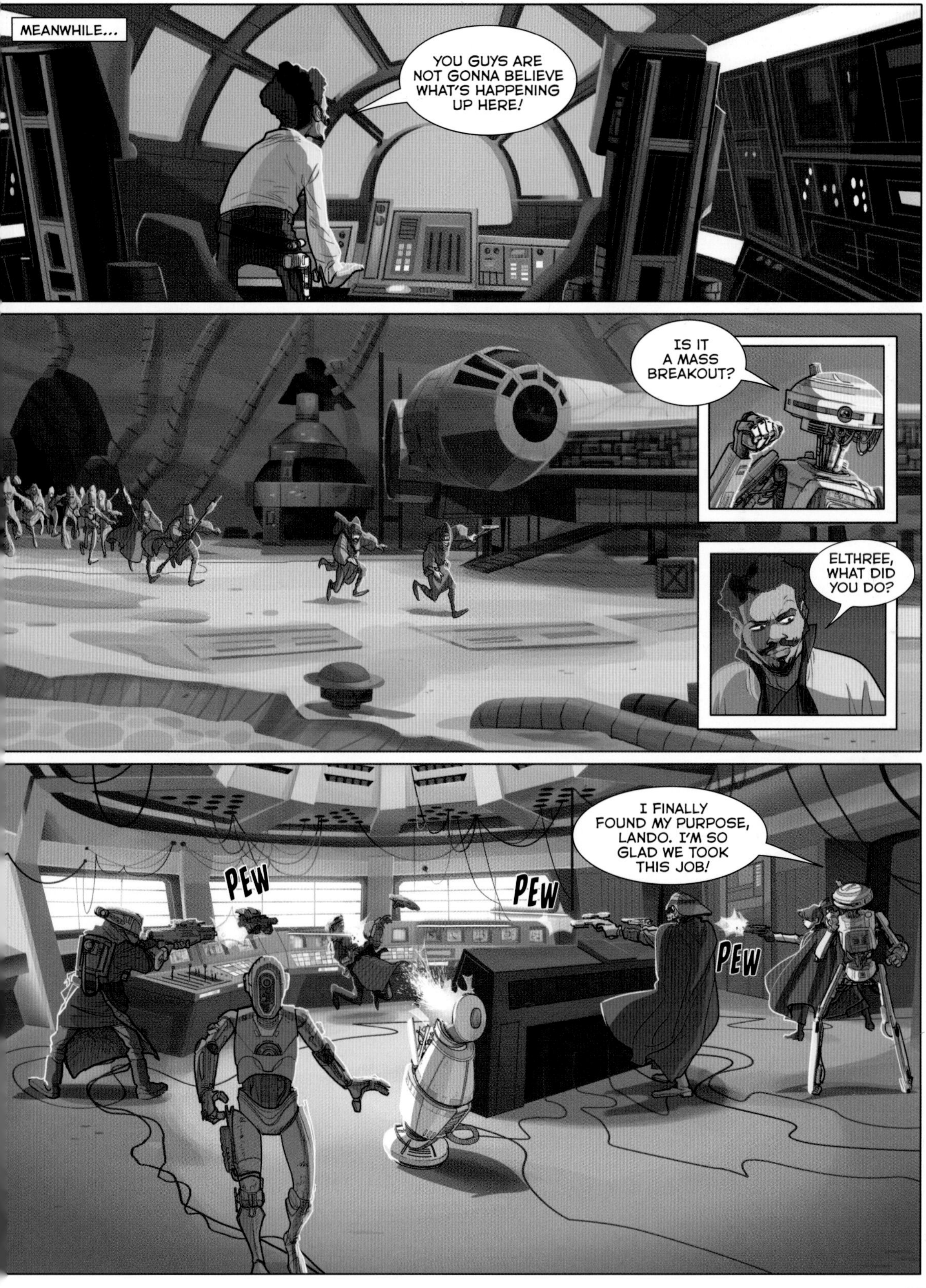
MEANWHILE...
YOU GUYS ARE NOT GONNA BELIEVE WHAT'S HAPPENING UP HERE!
IS IT A MASS BREAKOUT?
ELTHREE, WHAT DID YOU DO?
I FINALLY FOUND MY PURPOSE, LANDO. I'M SO GLAD WE TOOK THIS JOB!
PEW
PEW
PEW

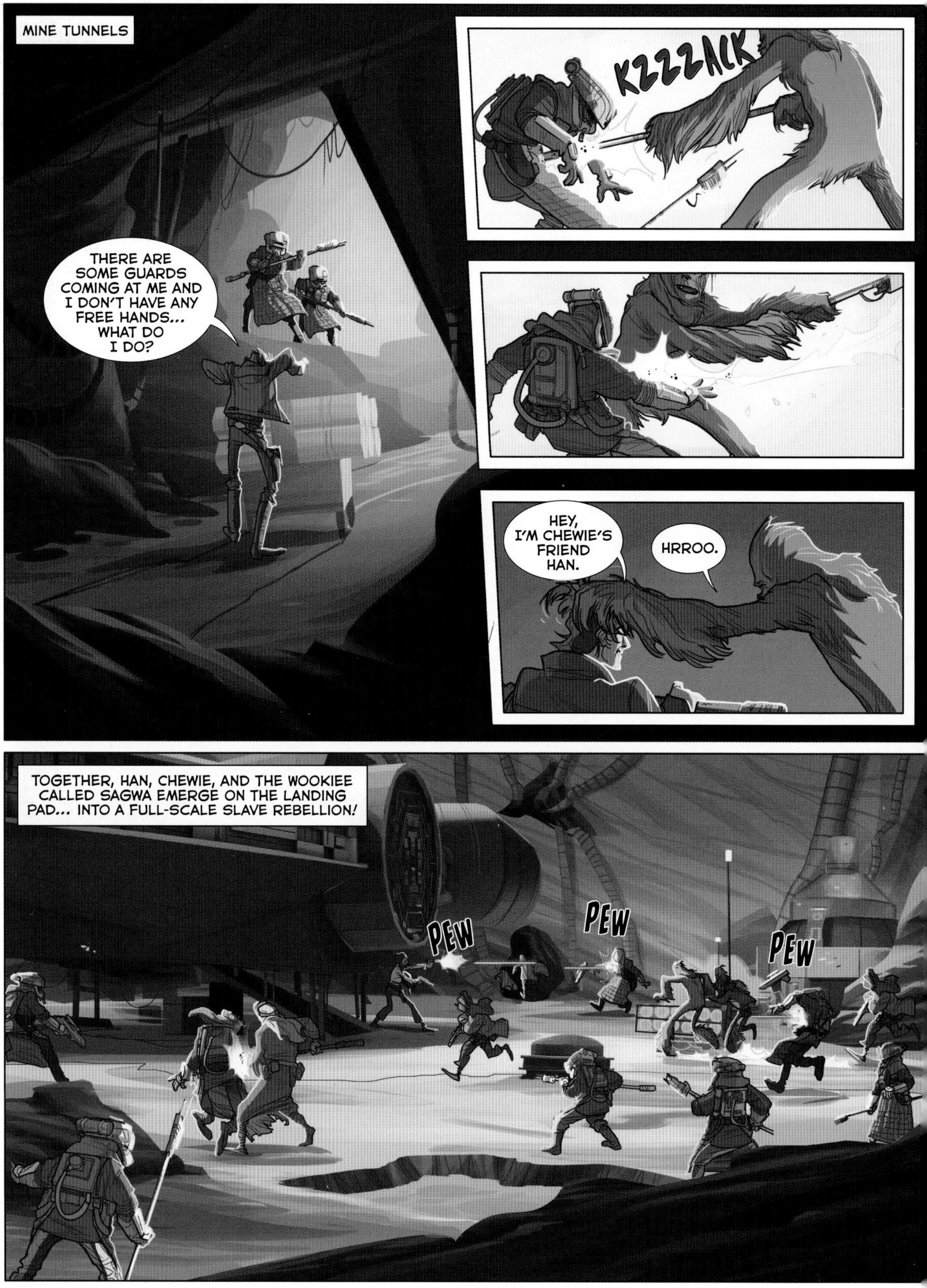
MINE TUNNELS
KZZZACK
THERE ARE SOME GUARDS COMING AT ME AND I DON'T HAVE ANY FREE HANDS... WHAT DO I DO?
HEY, I'M CHEWIE'S FRIEND HAN.
HRROO.
TOGETHER, HAN, CHEWIE, AND THE WOOKIEE CALLED SAGWA EMERGE ON THE LANDING PAD... INTO A FULL-SCALE SLAVE REBELLION!
PEW
PEW
PEW

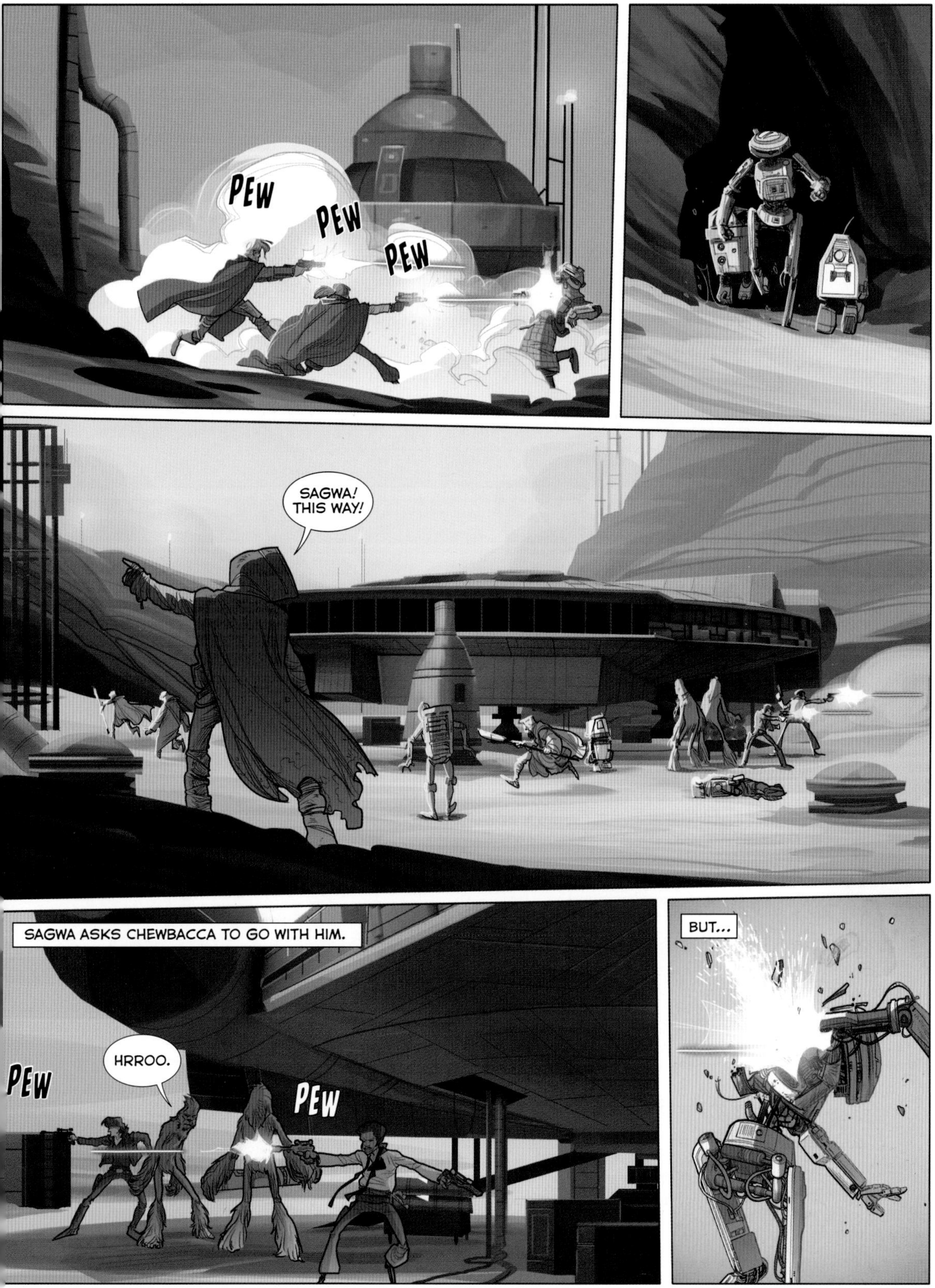
PEW
PEW
PEW
SAGWA! THIS WAY!
SAGWA ASKS CHEWBACCA TO GO WITH HIM.
PEW
HRROO.
PEW
BUT...

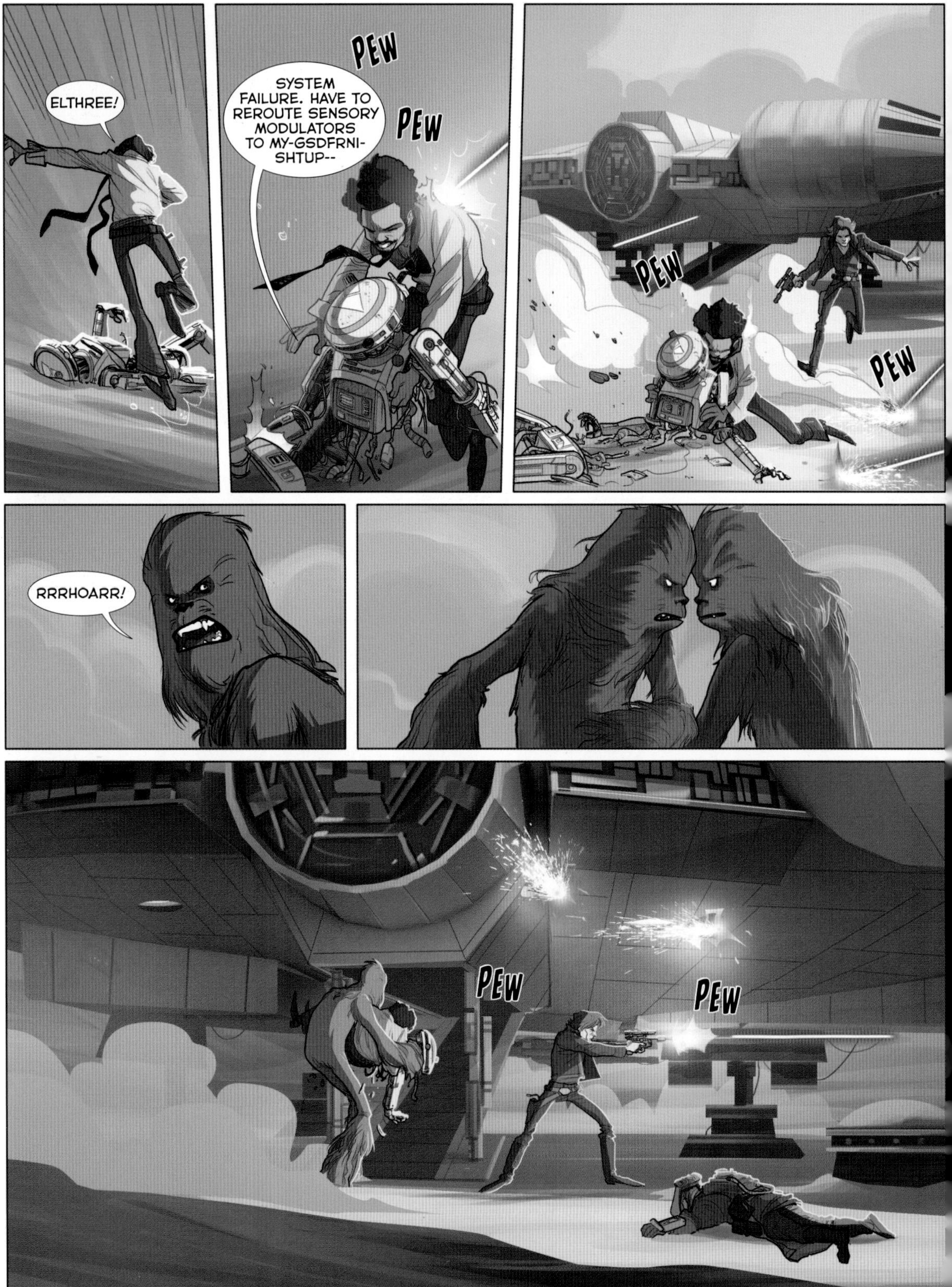
ELTHREE!
PEW
SYSTEM FAILURE. HAVE TO REROUTE SENSORY MODULATORS TO MY-GSDFRNI-SHTUP--
PEW
PEW
PEW
RRRHOARR!
PEW
PEW

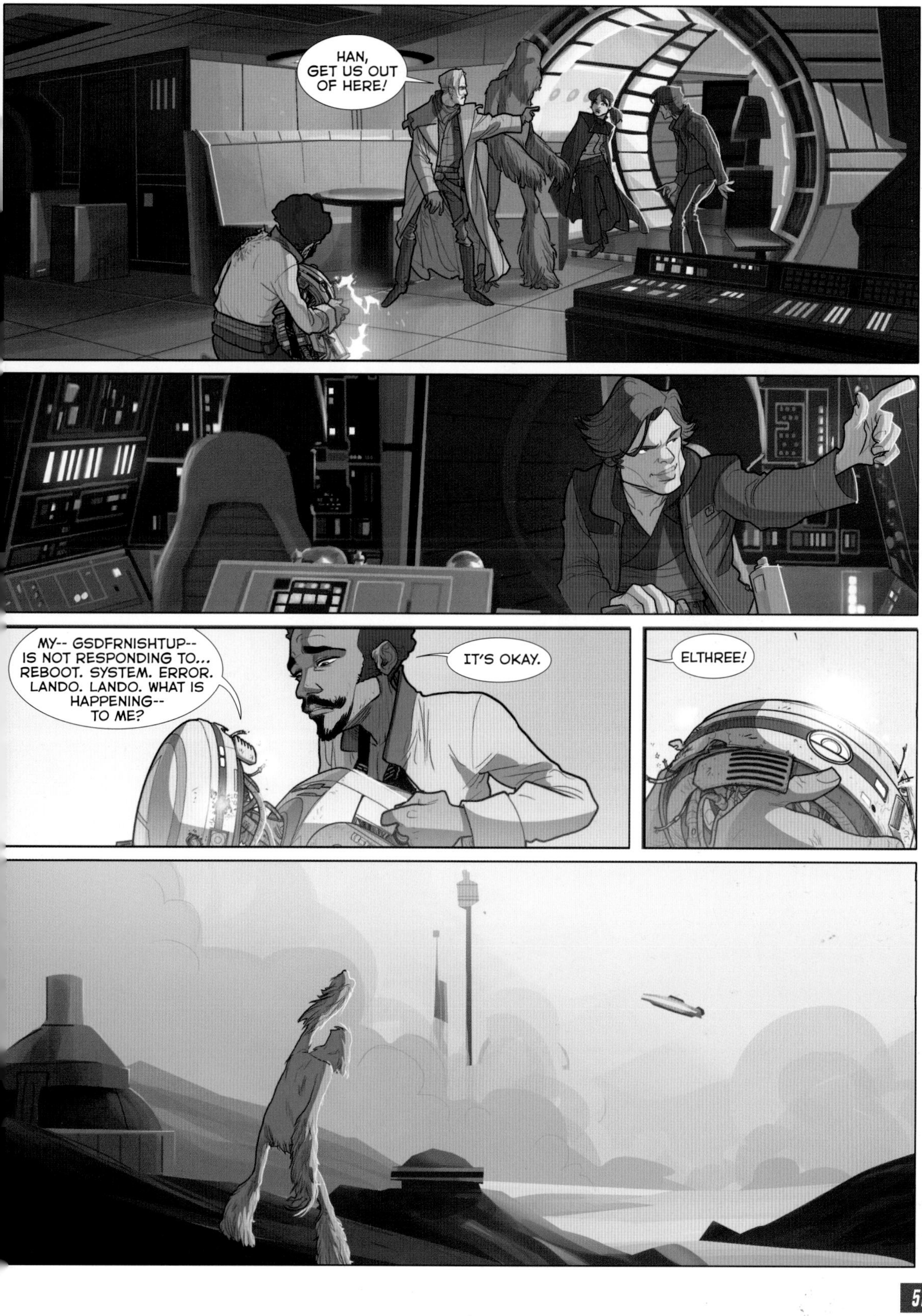
HAN, GET US OUT OF HERE!
MY-- GSDFRNISHTUP-- IS NOT RESPONDING TO... REBOOT. SYSTEM. ERROR. LANDO. LANDO. WHAT IS HAPPENING-- TO ME?
IT'S OKAY.
ELTHREE!

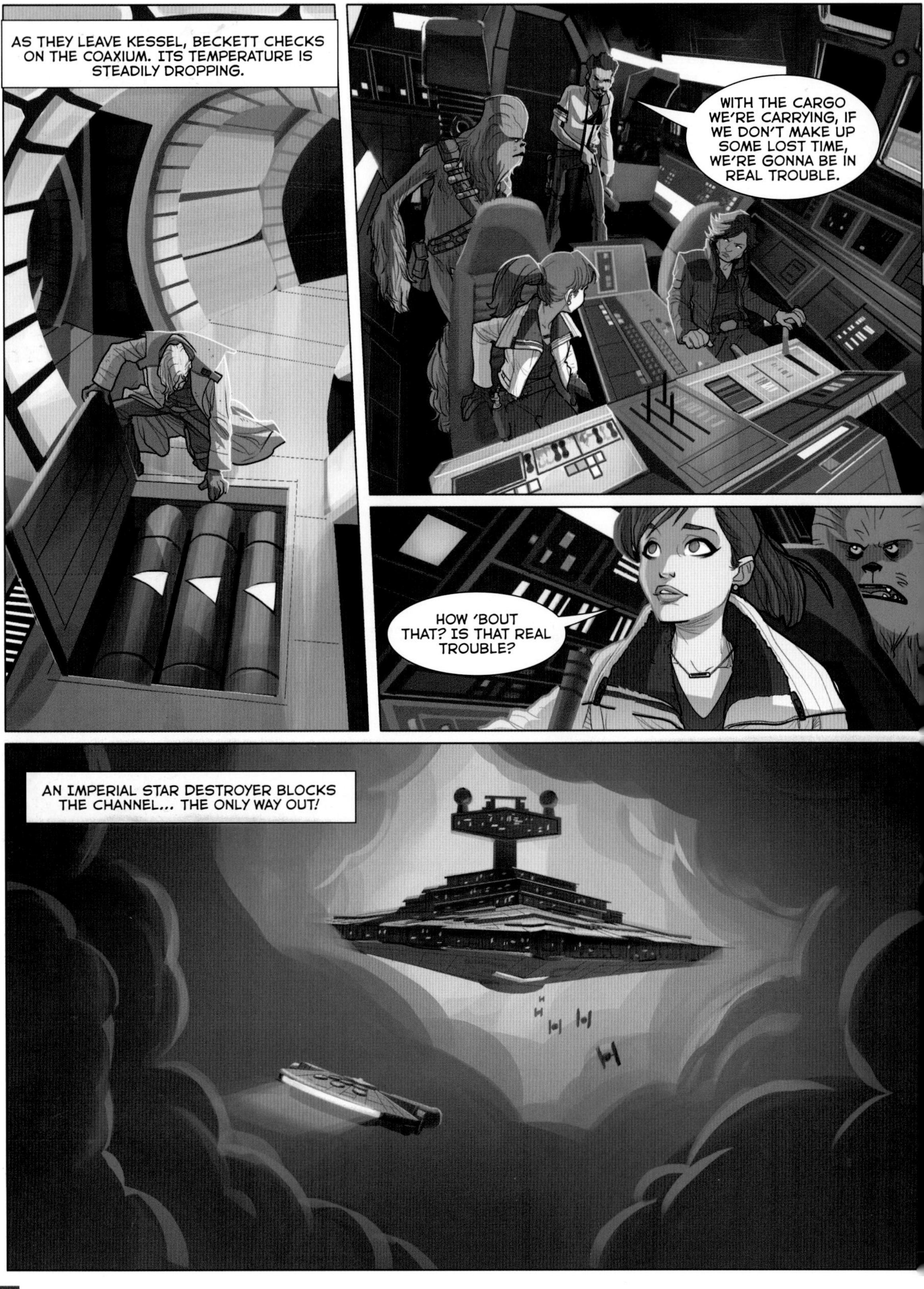

AS THEY LEAVE KESSEL, BECKETT CHECKS ON THE COAXIUM. ITS TEMPERATURE IS STEADILY DROPPING.
WITH THE CARGO WE'RE CARRYING, IF WE DON'T MAKE UP SOME LOST TIME, WE'RE GONNA BE IN REAL TROUBLE.
HOW 'BOUT THAT? IS THAT REAL TROUBLE?
AN IMPERIAL STAR DESTROYER BLOCKS THE CHANNEL... THE ONLY WAY OUT!

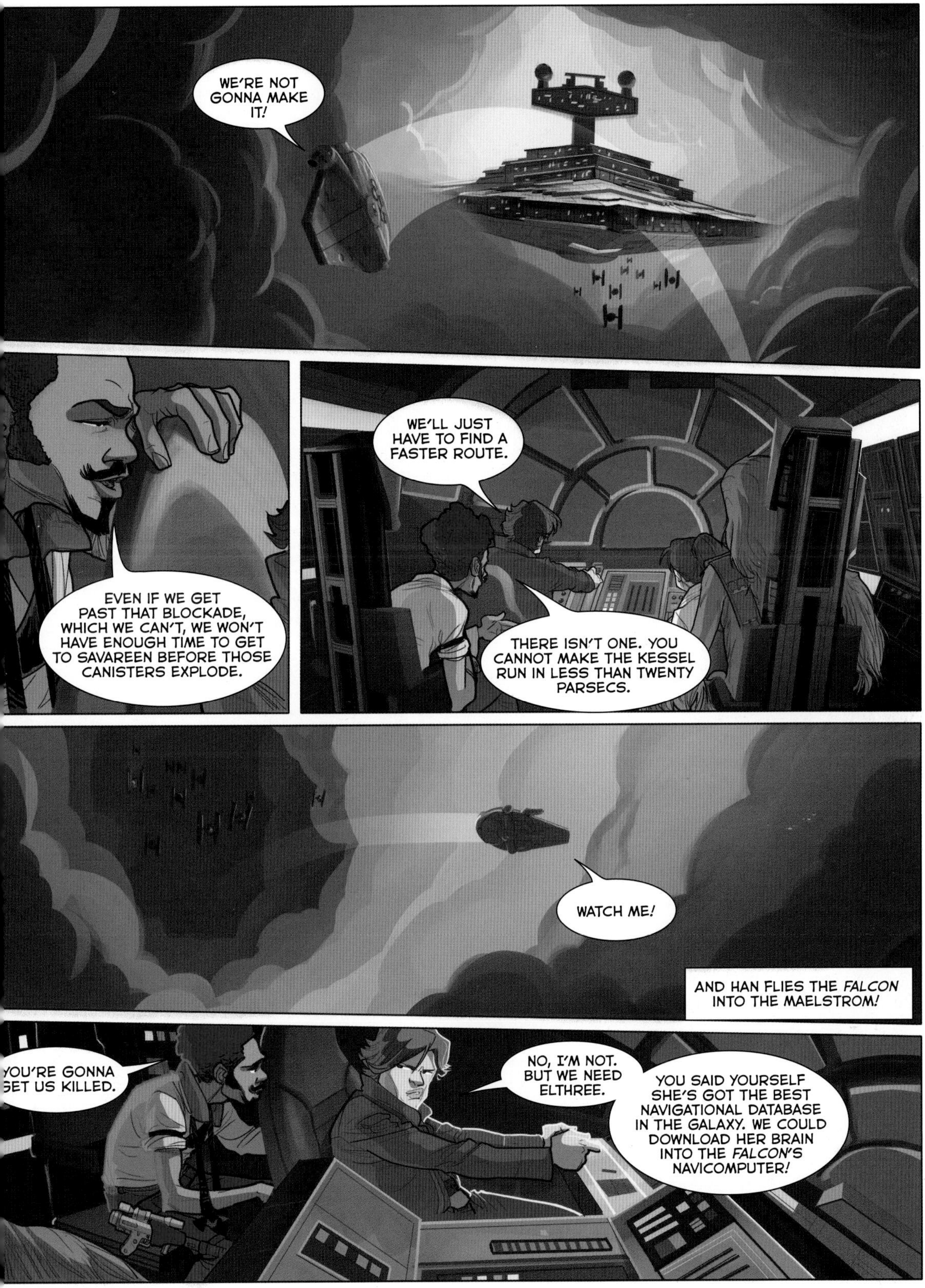

WE'RE NOT GONNA MAKE IT!
EVEN IF WE GET PAST THAT BLOCKADE, WHICH WE CAN'T, WE WON'T HAVE ENOUGH TIME TO GET TO SAVAREEN BEFORE THOSE CANISTERS EXPLODE.
WE'LL JUST HAVE TO FIND A FASTER ROUTE.
THERE ISN'T ONE. YOU CANNOT MAKE THE KESSEL RUN IN LESS THAN TWENTY PARSECS.
WATCH ME!
AND HAN FLIES THE *FALCON* INTO THE MAELSTROM!
YOU'RE GONNA GET US KILLED.
NO, I'M NOT. BUT WE NEED ELTHREE.
YOU SAID YOURSELF SHE'S GOT THE BEST NAVIGATIONAL DATABASE IN THE GALAXY. WE COULD DOWNLOAD HER BRAIN INTO THE *FALCON*'S NAVICOMPUTER!

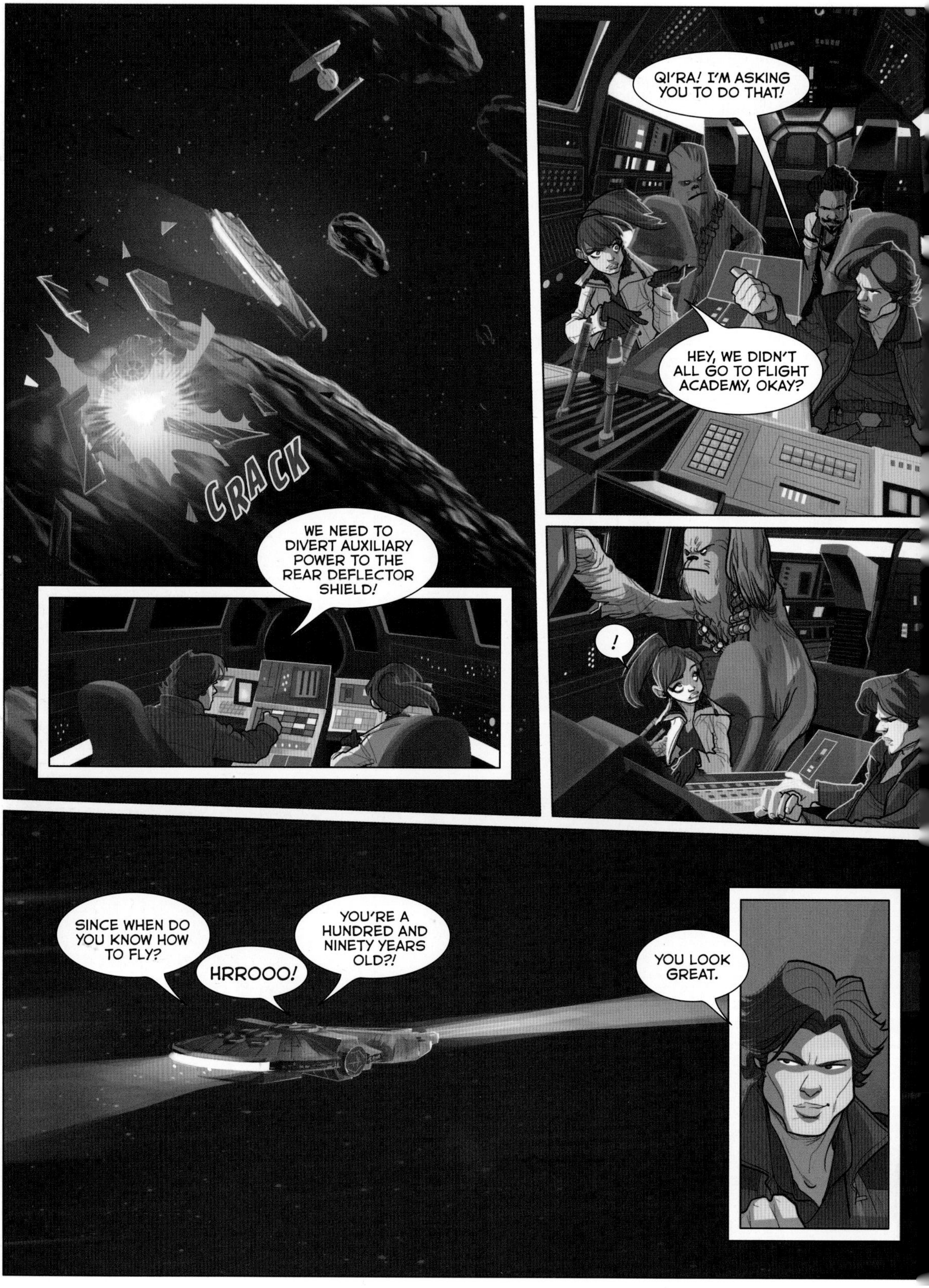
CRACK
QI'RA! I'M ASKING YOU TO DO THAT!
HEY, WE DIDN'T ALL GO TO FLIGHT ACADEMY, OKAY?
WE NEED TO DIVERT AUXILIARY POWER TO THE REAR DEFLECTOR SHIELD!
!
SINCE WHEN DO YOU KNOW HOW TO FLY?
HRROOO!
YOU'RE A HUNDRED AND NINETY YEARS OLD?!
YOU LOOK GREAT.

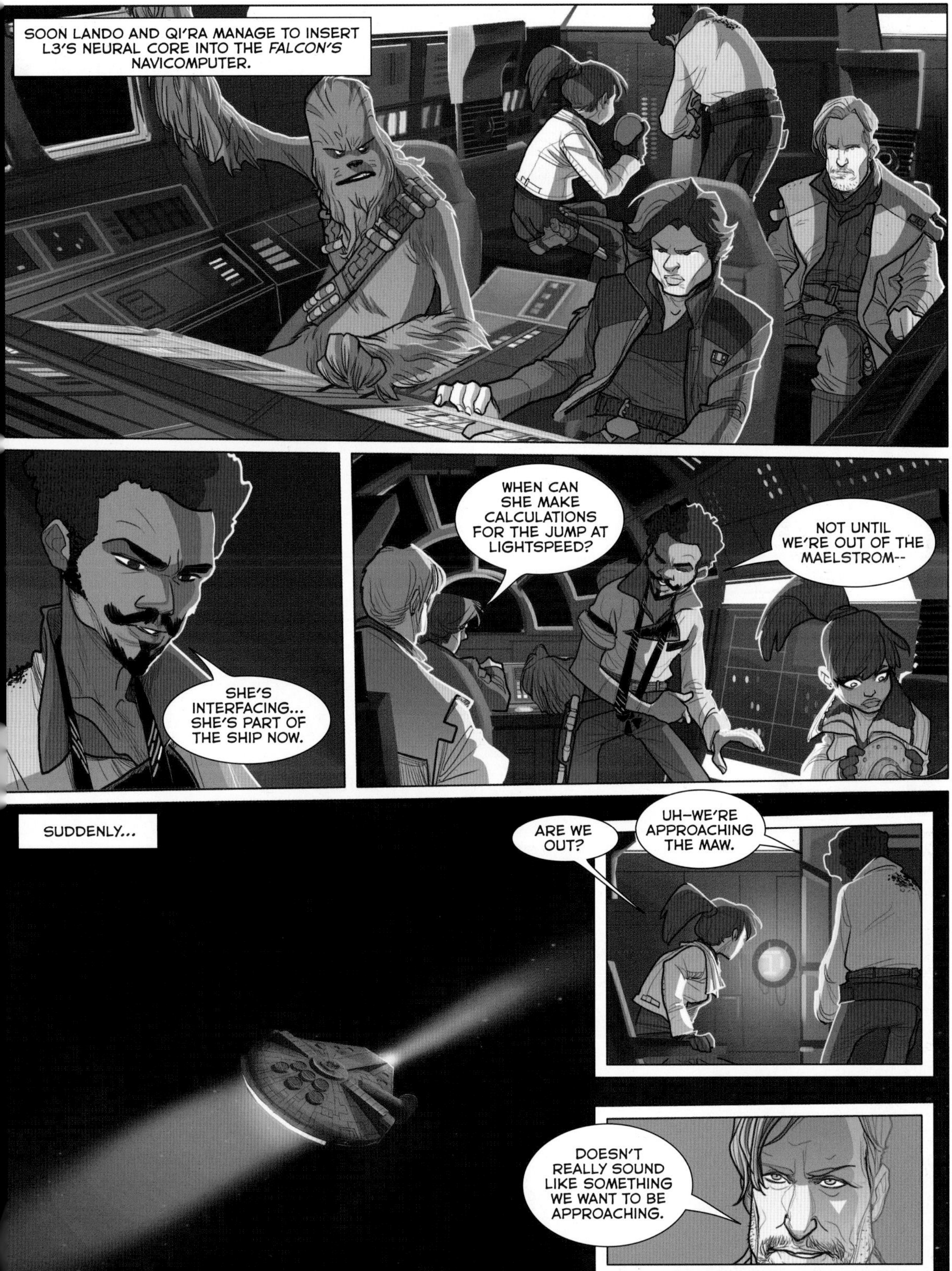
SOON LANDO AND QI'RA MANAGE TO INSERT L3'S NEURAL CORE INTO THE *FALCON'S* NAVICOMPUTER.
SHE'S INTERFACING... SHE'S PART OF THE SHIP NOW.
WHEN CAN SHE MAKE CALCULATIONS FOR THE JUMP AT LIGHTSPEED?
NOT UNTIL WE'RE OUT OF THE MAELSTROM--
SUDDENLY...
ARE WE OUT?
UH-WE'RE APPROACHING THE MAW.
DOESN'T REALLY SOUND LIKE SOMETHING WE WANT TO BE APPROACHING.

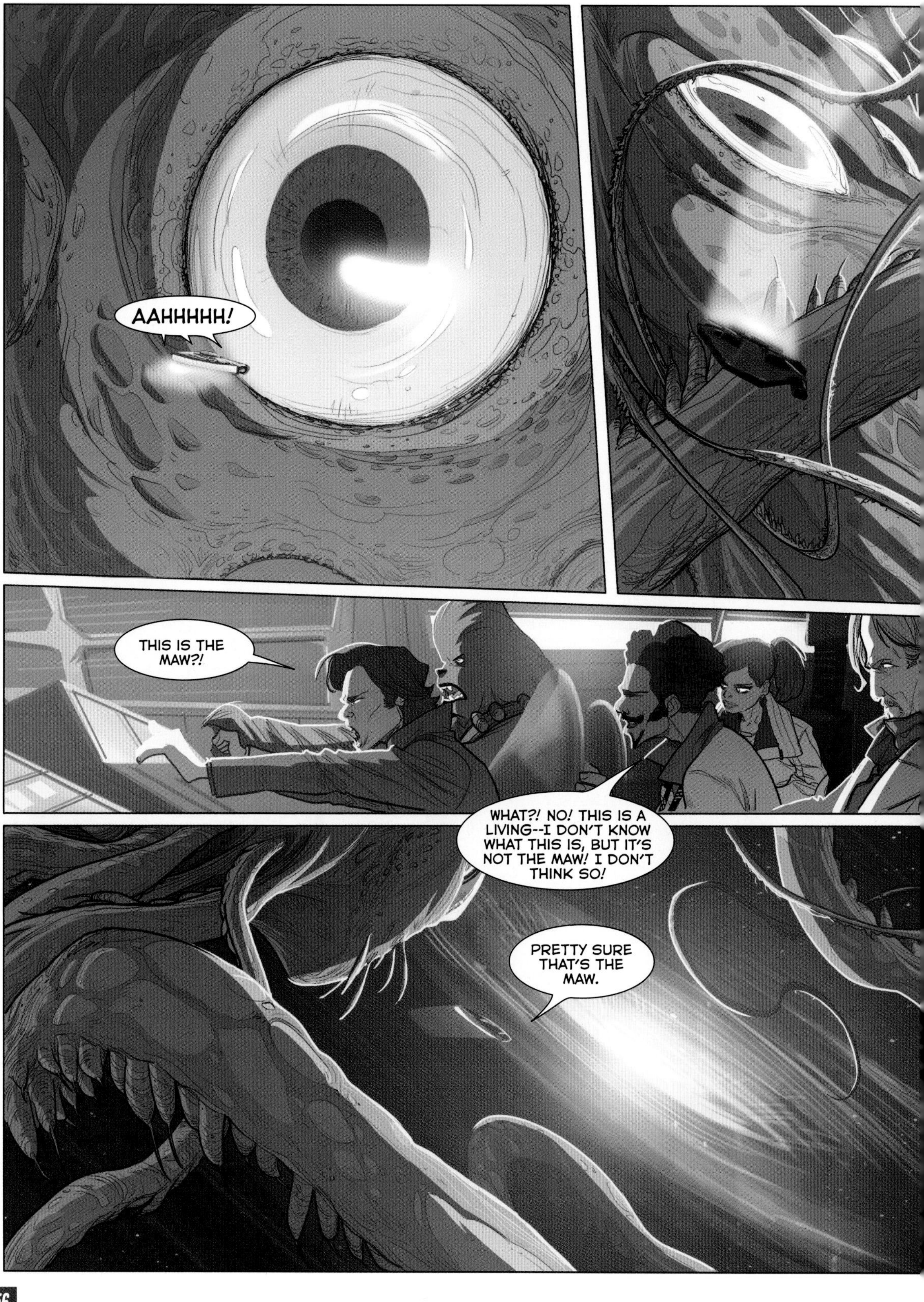
AAHHHHH!
THIS IS THE MAW?!
WHAT?! NO! THIS IS A LIVING--I DON'T KNOW WHAT THIS IS, BUT IT'S NOT THE MAW! I DON'T THINK SO!
PRETTY SURE THAT'S THE MAW.

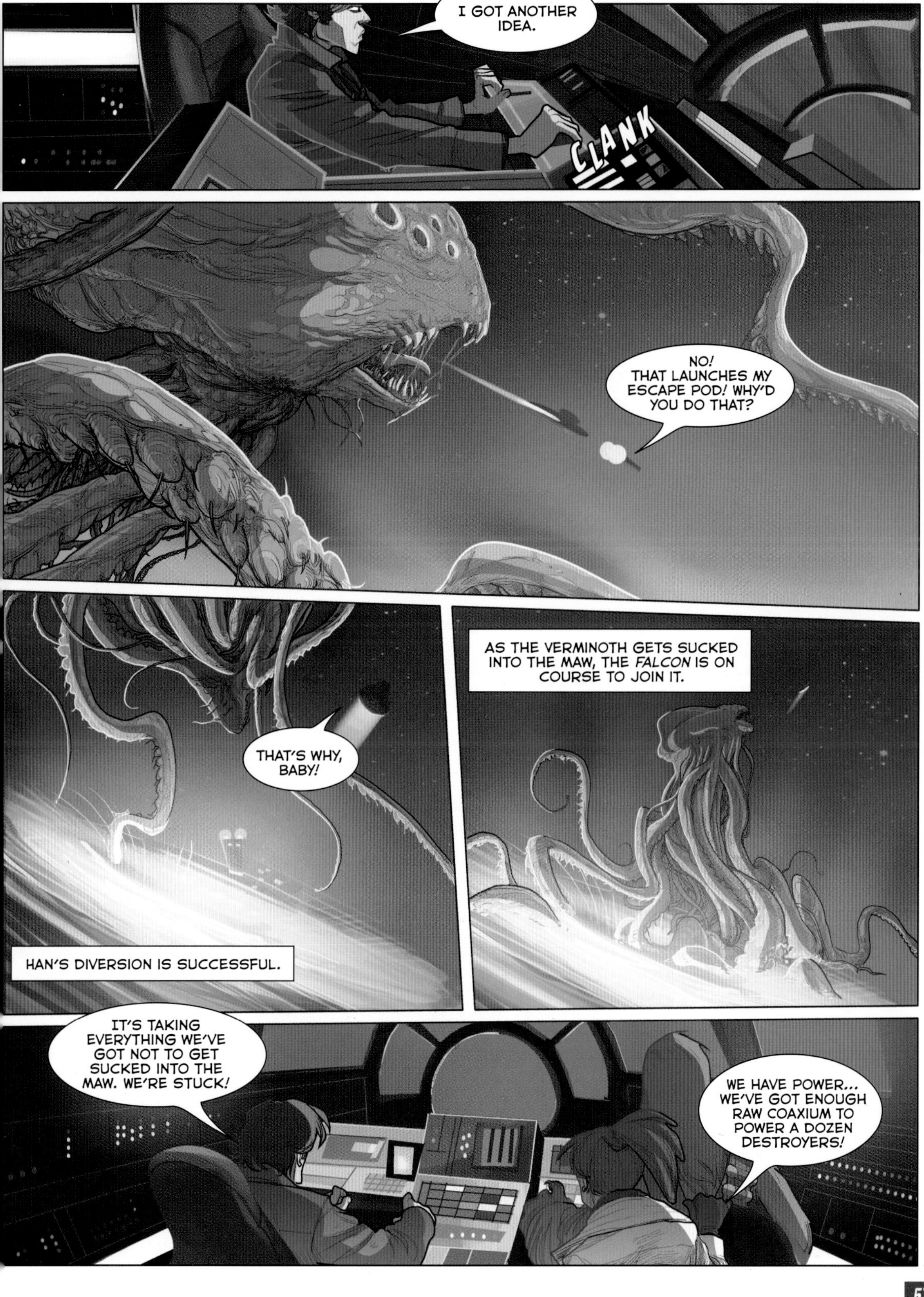
I GOT ANOTHER IDEA.
CLANK
NO! THAT LAUNCHES MY ESCAPE POD! WHY'D YOU DO THAT?
THAT'S WHY, BABY!
HAN'S DIVERSION IS SUCCESSFUL.
AS THE VERMINOTH GETS SUCKED INTO THE MAW, THE *FALCON* IS ON COURSE TO JOIN IT.
IT'S TAKING EVERYTHING WE'VE GOT NOT TO GET SUCKED INTO THE MAW. WE'RE STUCK!
WE HAVE POWER... WE'VE GOT ENOUGH RAW COAXIUM TO POWER A DOZEN DESTROYERS!

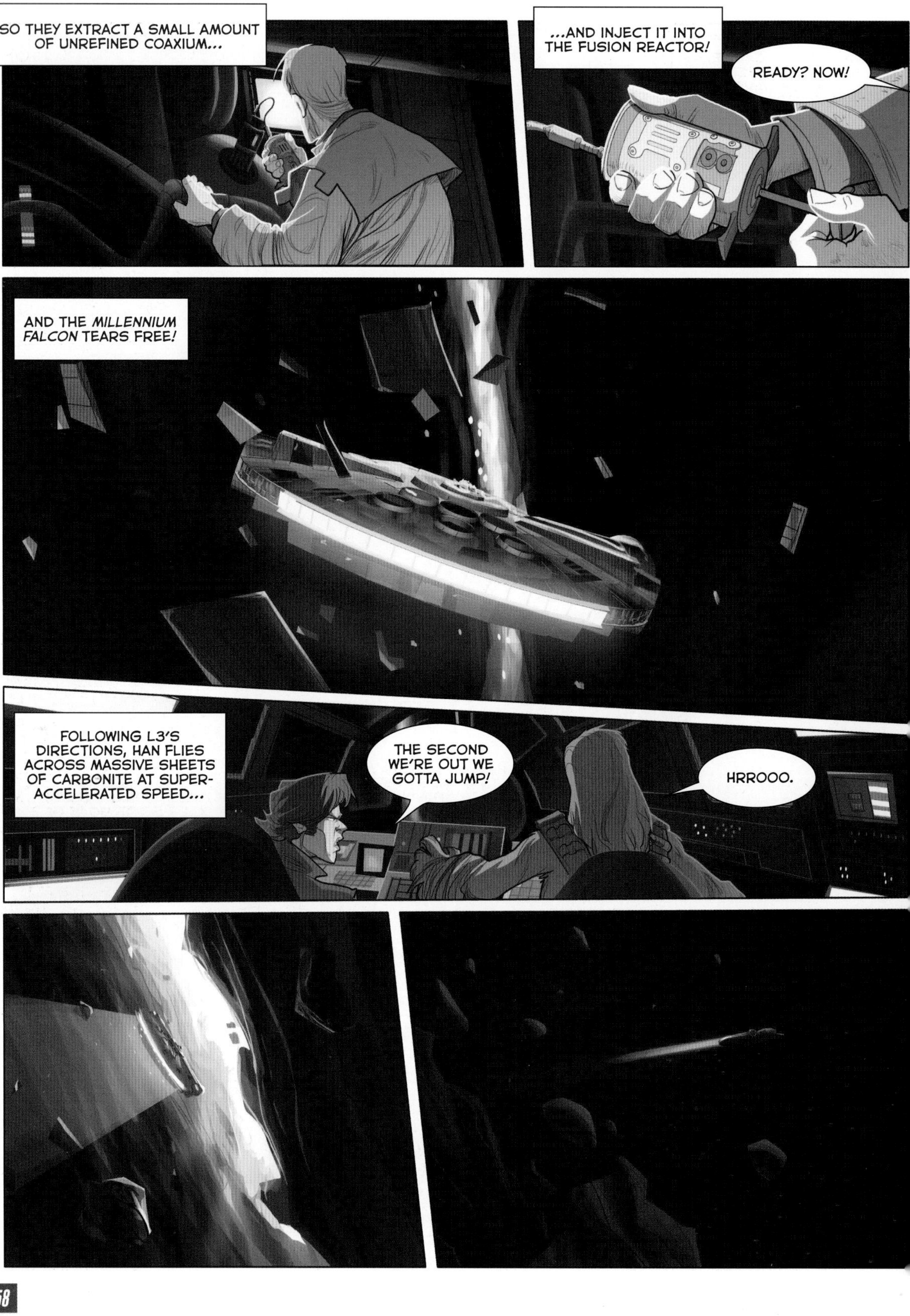
SO THEY EXTRACT A SMALL AMOUNT OF UNREFINED COAXIUM...
...AND INJECT IT INTO THE FUSION REACTOR!
READY? NOW!
AND THE *MILLENNIUM FALCON* TEARS FREE!
FOLLOWING L3'S DIRECTIONS, HAN FLIES ACROSS MASSIVE SHEETS OF CARBONITE AT SUPER-ACCELERATED SPEED...
THE SECOND WE'RE OUT WE GOTTA JUMP!
HRROOO.

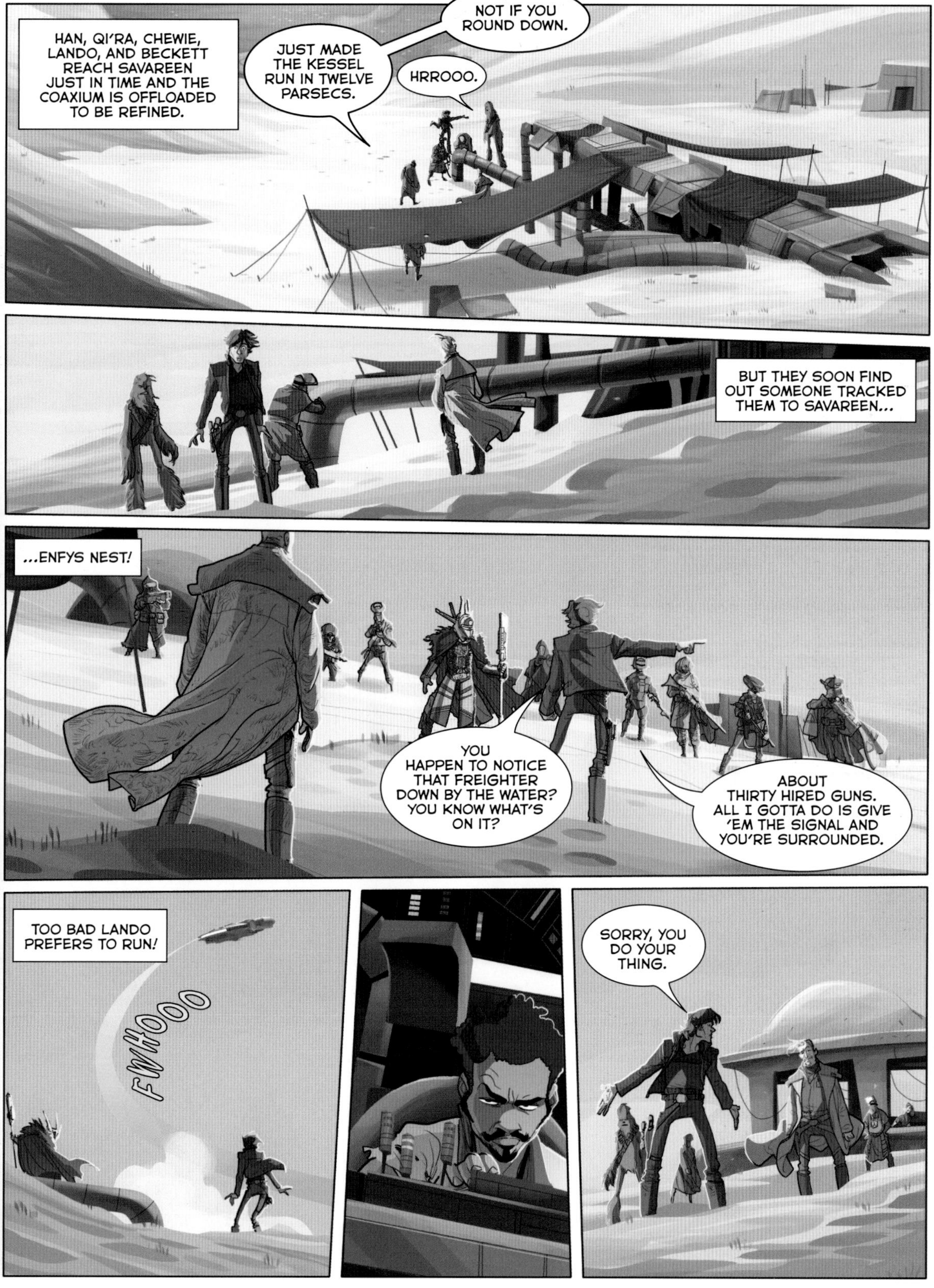
HAN, QI'RA, CHEWIE, LANDO, AND BECKETT REACH SAVAREEN JUST IN TIME AND THE COAXIUM IS OFFLOADED TO BE REFINED.
JUST MADE THE KESSEL RUN IN TWELVE PARSECS.
NOT IF YOU ROUND DOWN.
HRROOO.
BUT THEY SOON FIND OUT SOMEONE TRACKED THEM TO SAVAREEN...
...ENFYS NEST!
YOU HAPPEN TO NOTICE THAT FREIGHTER DOWN BY THE WATER? YOU KNOW WHAT'S ON IT?
ABOUT THIRTY HIRED GUNS. ALL I GOTTA DO IS GIVE 'EM THE SIGNAL AND YOU'RE SURROUNDED.
TOO BAD LANDO PREFERS TO RUN!
FWHOOO
SORRY, YOU DO YOUR THING.

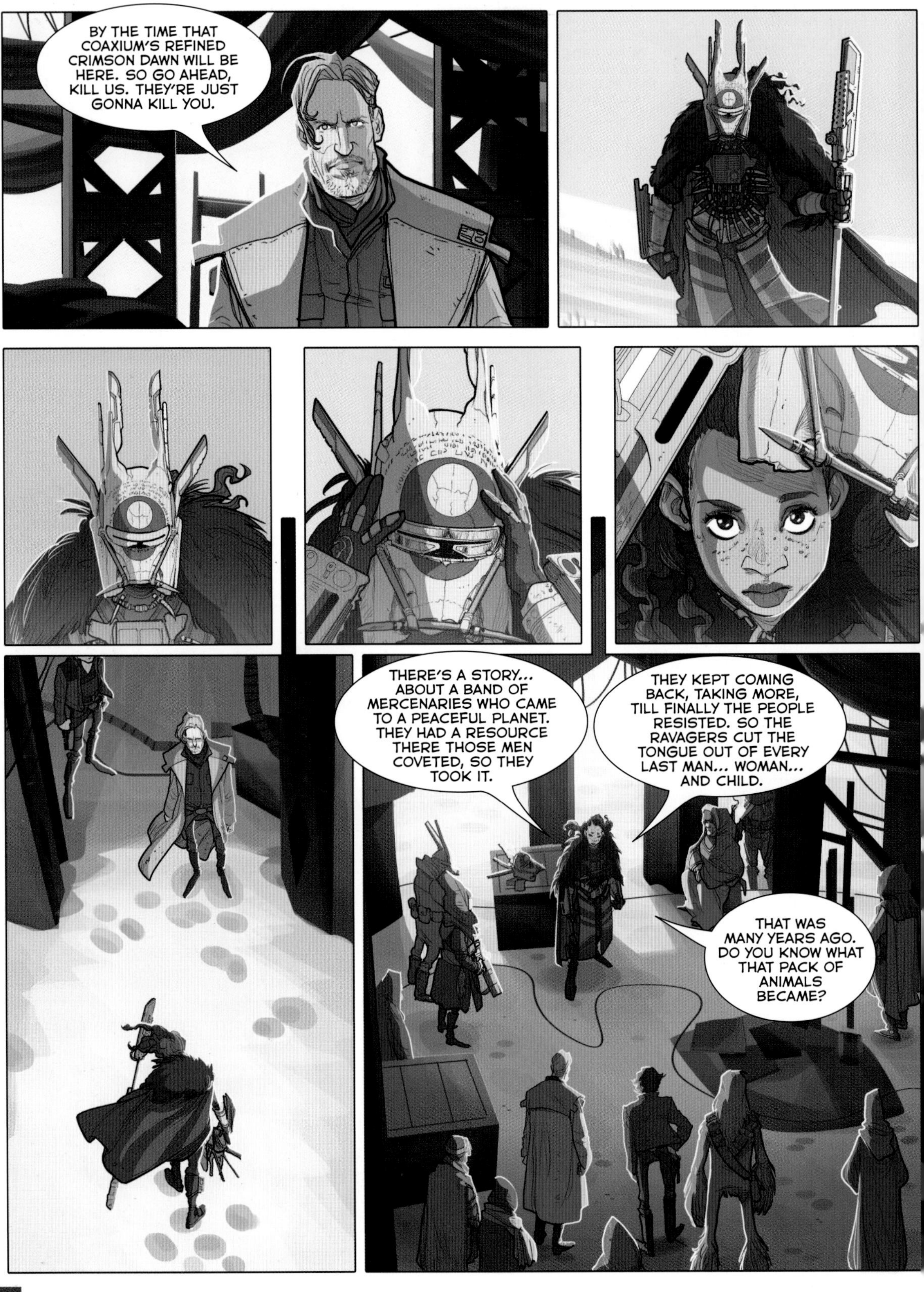
BY THE TIME THAT COAXIUM'S REFINED CRIMSON DAWN WILL BE HERE. SO GO AHEAD, KILL US. THEY'RE JUST GONNA KILL YOU.
THERE'S A STORY... ABOUT A BAND OF MERCENARIES WHO CAME TO A PEACEFUL PLANET. THEY HAD A RESOURCE THERE THOSE MEN COVETED, SO THEY TOOK IT.
THEY KEPT COMING BACK, TAKING MORE, TILL FINALLY THE PEOPLE RESISTED. SO THE RAVAGERS CUT THE TONGUE OUT OF EVERY LAST MAN... WOMAN... AND CHILD.
THAT WAS MANY YEARS AGO. DO YOU KNOW WHAT THAT PACK OF ANIMALS BECAME?

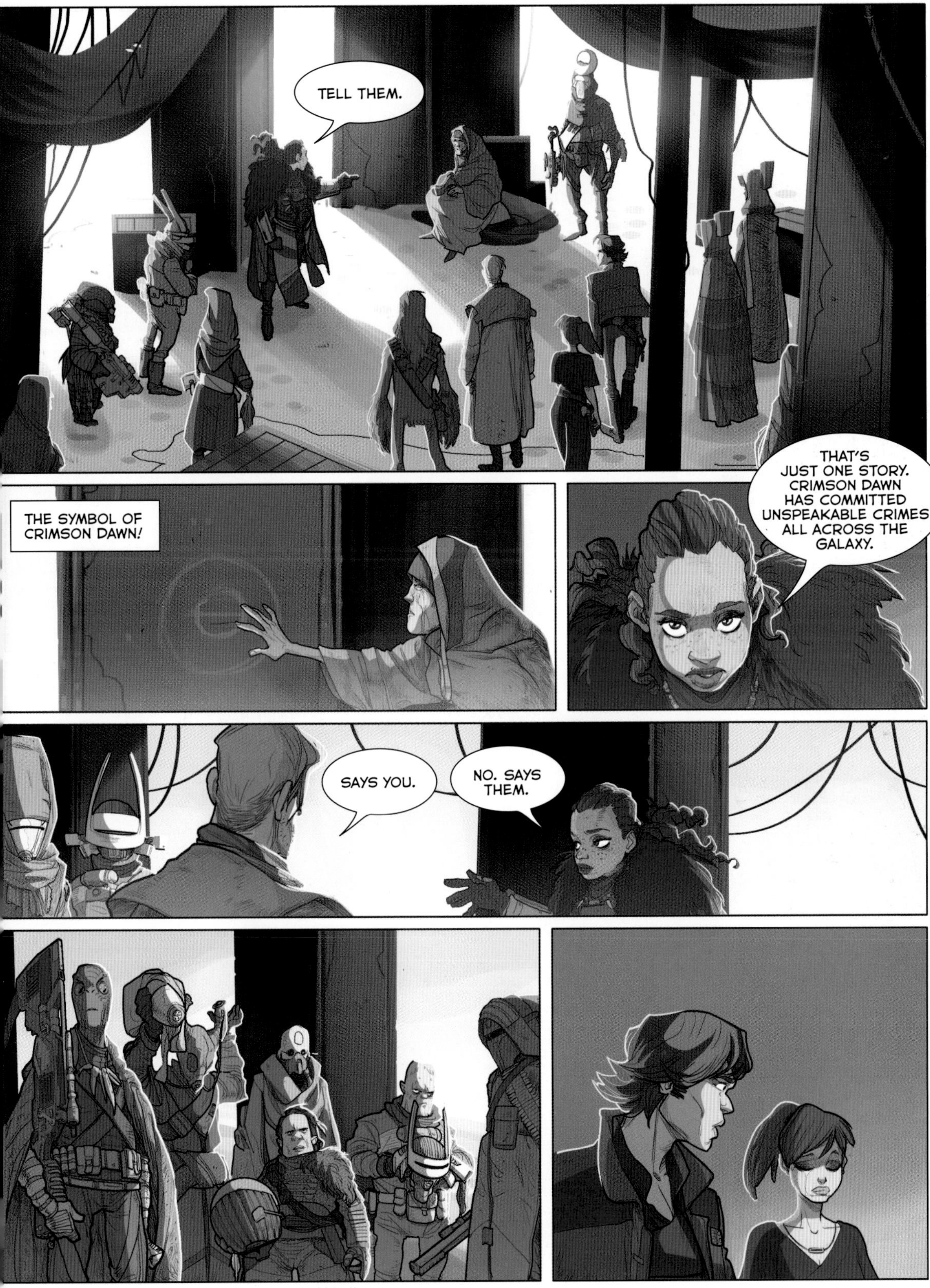
TELL THEM.
THE SYMBOL OF CRIMSON DAWN!
THAT'S JUST ONE STORY. CRIMSON DAWN HAS COMMITTED UNSPEAKABLE CRIMES ALL ACROSS THE GALAXY.
SAYS YOU.
NO. SAYS THEM.

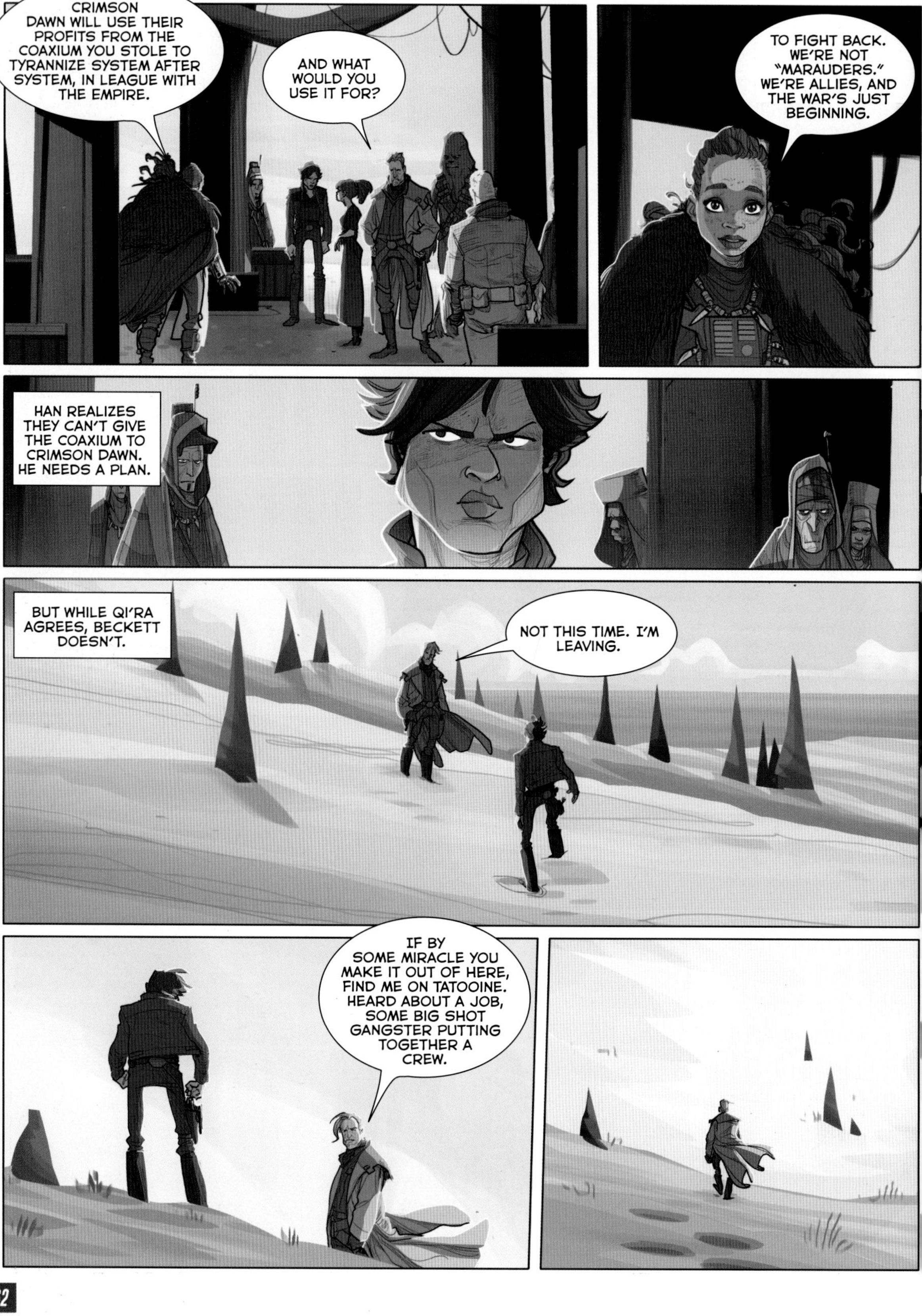

CRIMSON DAWN WILL USE THEIR PROFITS FROM THE COAXIUM YOU STOLE TO TYRANNIZE SYSTEM AFTER SYSTEM, IN LEAGUE WITH THE EMPIRE.
AND WHAT WOULD YOU USE IT FOR?
TO FIGHT BACK. WE'RE NOT "MARAUDERS." WE'RE ALLIES, AND THE WAR'S JUST BEGINNING.
HAN REALIZES THEY CAN'T GIVE THE COAXIUM TO CRIMSON DAWN. HE NEEDS A PLAN.
BUT WHILE QI'RA AGREES, BECKETT DOESN'T.
NOT THIS TIME. I'M LEAVING.
IF BY SOME MIRACLE YOU MAKE IT OUT OF HERE, FIND ME ON TATOOINE. HEARD ABOUT A JOB, SOME BIG SHOT GANGSTER PUTTING TOGETHER A CREW.

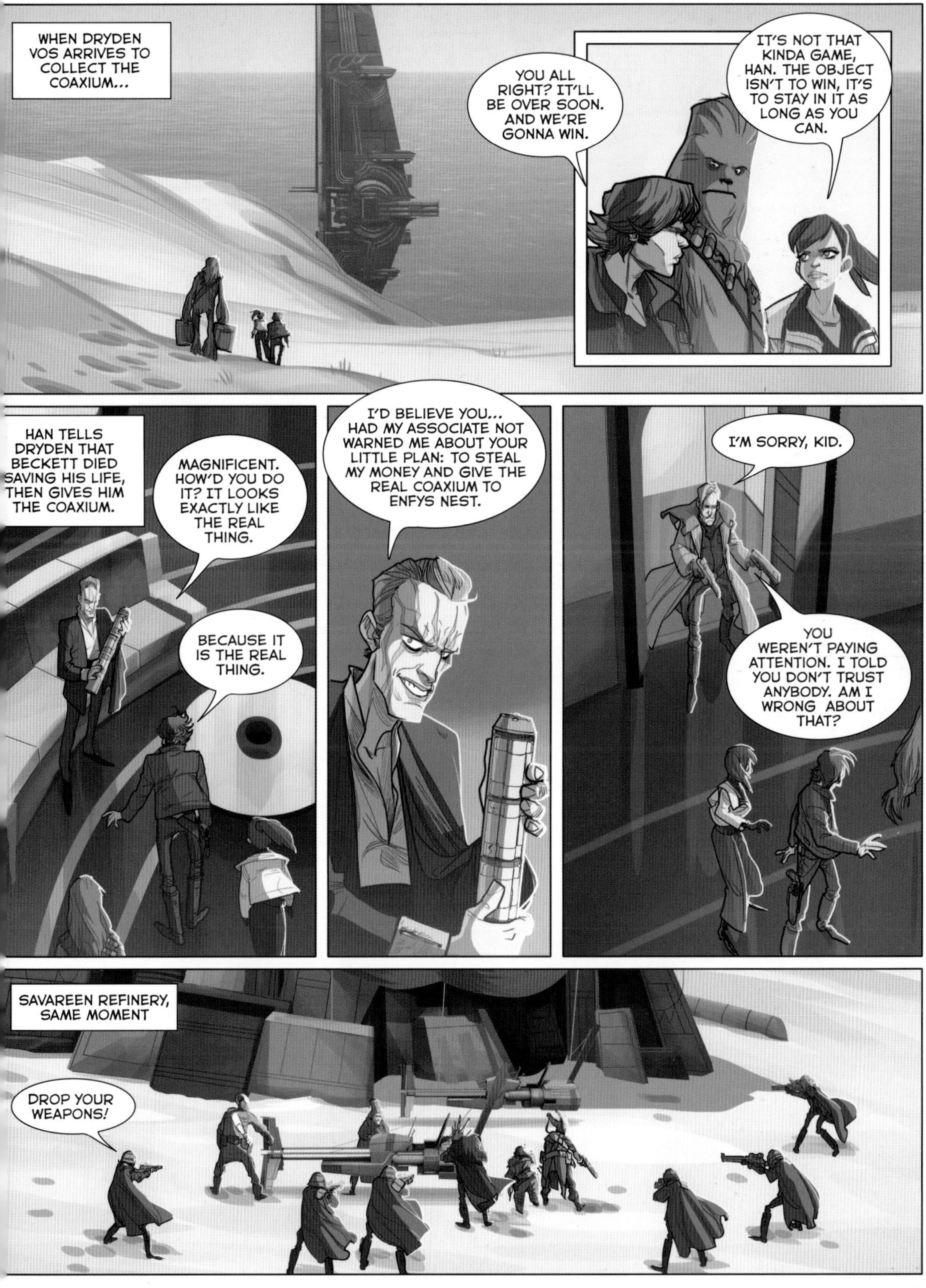
WHEN DRYDEN VOS ARRIVES TO COLLECT THE COAXIUM...
YOU ALL RIGHT? IT'LL BE OVER SOON. AND WE'RE GONNA WIN.
IT'S NOT THAT KINDA GAME, HAN. THE OBJECT ISN'T TO WIN, IT'S TO STAY IN IT AS LONG AS YOU CAN.
HAN TELLS DRYDEN THAT BECKETT DIED SAVING HIS LIFE, THEN GIVES HIM THE COAXIUM.
MAGNIFICENT. HOW'D YOU DO IT? IT LOOKS EXACTLY LIKE THE REAL THING.
BECAUSE IT IS THE REAL THING.
I'D BELIEVE YOU... HAD MY ASSOCIATE NOT WARNED ME ABOUT YOUR LITTLE PLAN: TO STEAL MY MONEY AND GIVE THE REAL COAXIUM TO ENFYS NEST.
I'M SORRY, KID.
YOU WEREN'T PAYING ATTENTION. I TOLD YOU DON'T TRUST ANYBODY. AM I WRONG ABOUT THAT?
SAVAREEN REFINERY, SAME MOMENT
DROP YOUR WEAPONS!

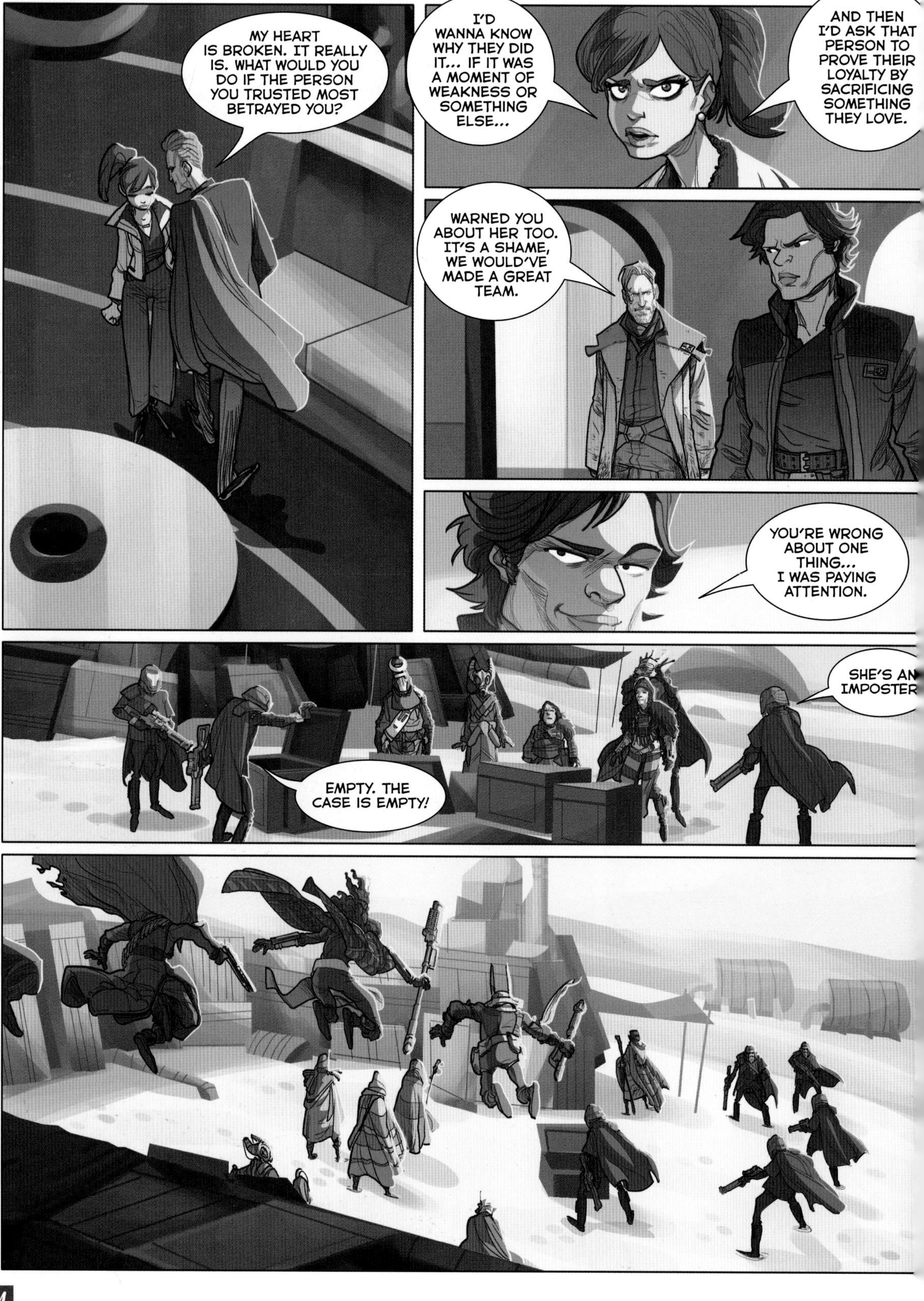
MY HEART IS BROKEN. IT REALLY IS. WHAT WOULD YOU DO IF THE PERSON YOU TRUSTED MOST BETRAYED YOU?
I'D WANNA KNOW WHY THEY DID IT... IF IT WAS A MOMENT OF WEAKNESS OR SOMETHING ELSE...
AND THEN I'D ASK THAT PERSON TO PROVE THEIR LOYALTY BY SACRIFICING SOMETHING THEY LOVE.
WARNED YOU ABOUT HER TOO. IT'S A SHAME, WE WOULD'VE MADE A GREAT TEAM.
YOU'RE WRONG ABOUT ONE THING... I WAS PAYING ATTENTION.
SHE'S AN IMPOSTER
EMPTY. THE CASE IS EMPTY!

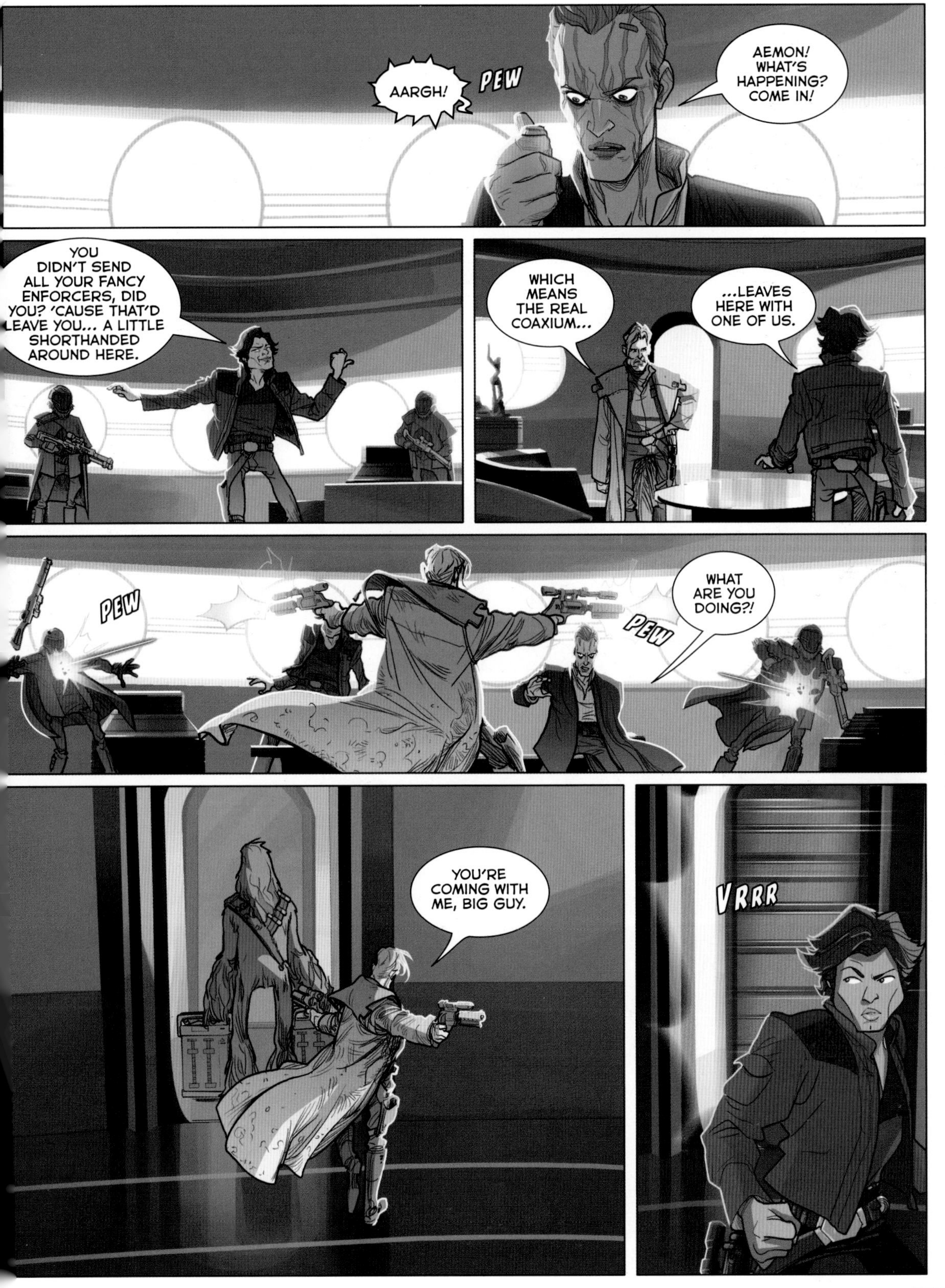
AARGH!
PEW
AEMON! WHAT'S HAPPENING? COME IN!
YOU DIDN'T SEND ALL YOUR FANCY ENFORCERS, DID YOU? 'CAUSE THAT'D LEAVE YOU... A LITTLE SHORTHANDED AROUND HERE.
WHICH MEANS THE REAL COAXIUM...
...LEAVES HERE WITH ONE OF US.
PEW
PEW
WHAT ARE YOU DOING?!
YOU'RE COMING WITH ME, BIG GUY.
VRRR

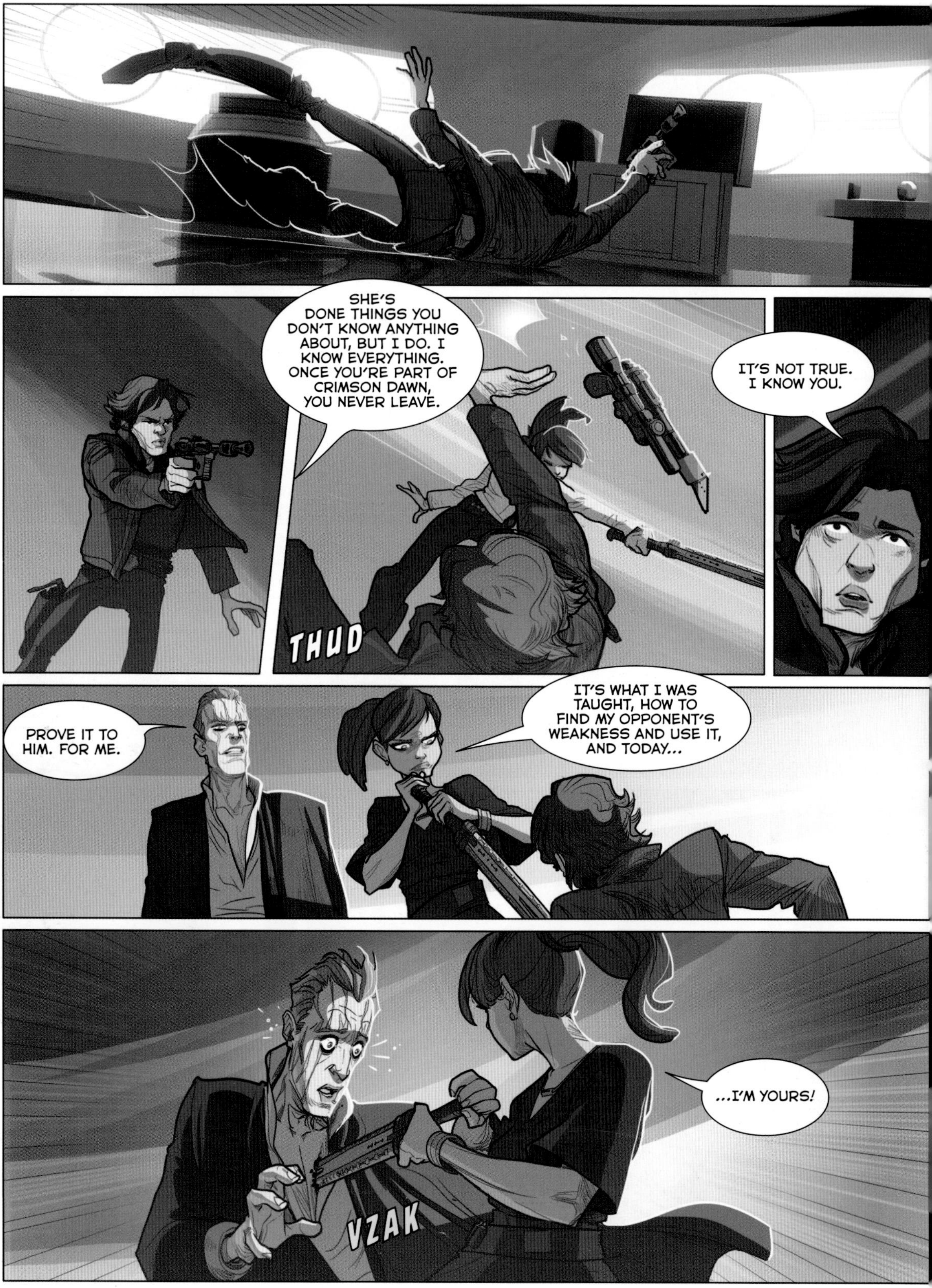
SHE'S DONE THINGS YOU DON'T KNOW ANYTHING ABOUT, BUT I DO. I KNOW EVERYTHING. ONCE YOU'RE PART OF CRIMSON DAWN, YOU NEVER LEAVE.
THUD
IT'S NOT TRUE. I KNOW YOU.
PROVE IT TO HIM. FOR ME.
IT'S WHAT I WAS TAUGHT, HOW TO FIND MY OPPONENT'S WEAKNESS AND USE IT, AND TODAY...
...I'M YOURS!
VZAK

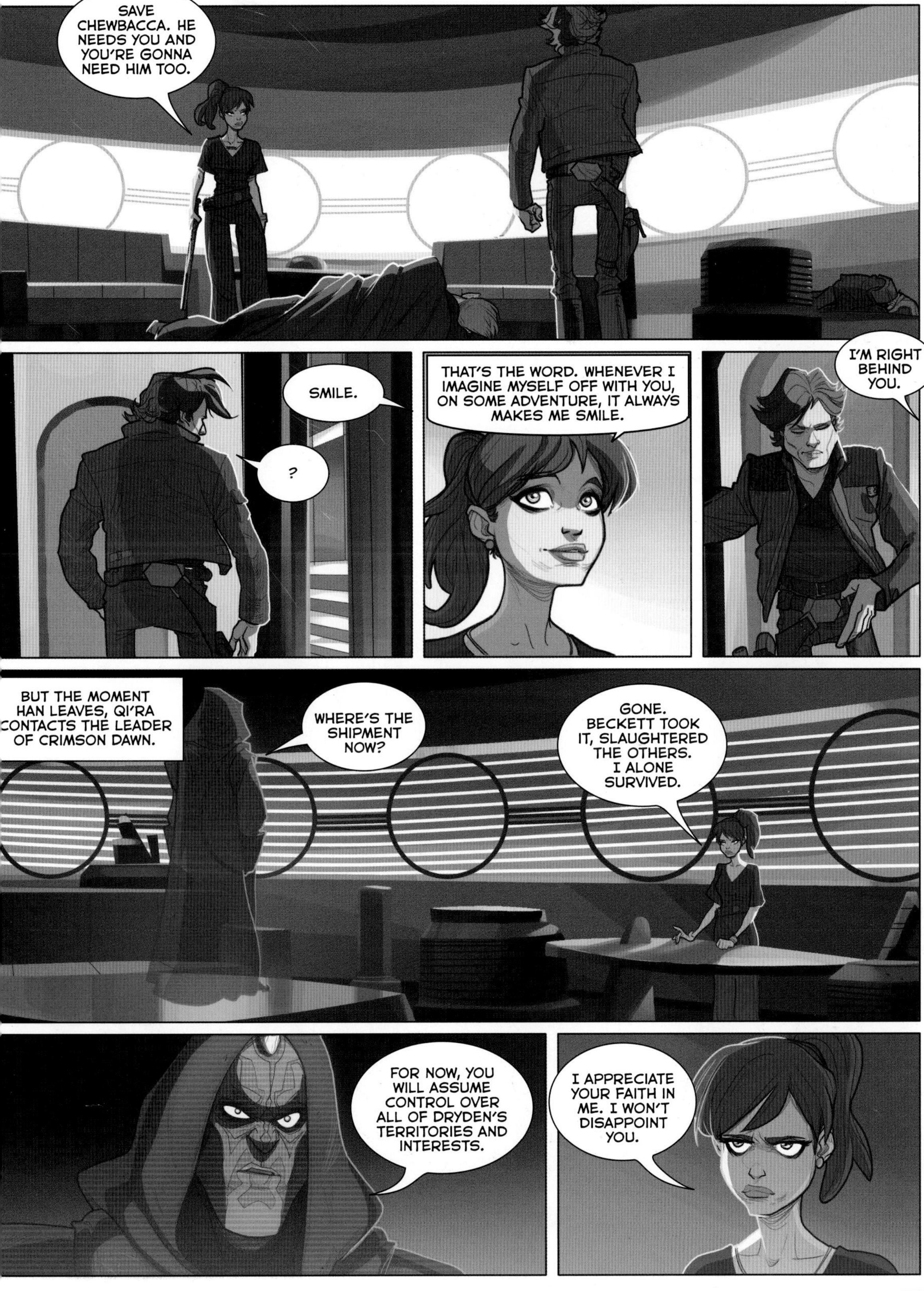
SAVE CHEWBACCA. HE NEEDS YOU AND YOU'RE GONNA NEED HIM TOO.
SMILE.
?
THAT'S THE WORD. WHENEVER I IMAGINE MYSELF OFF WITH YOU, ON SOME ADVENTURE, IT ALWAYS MAKES ME SMILE.
I'M RIGHT BEHIND YOU.
BUT THE MOMENT HAN LEAVES, QI'RA CONTACTS THE LEADER OF CRIMSON DAWN.
WHERE'S THE SHIPMENT NOW?
GONE. BECKETT TOOK IT, SLAUGHTERED THE OTHERS. I ALONE SURVIVED.
FOR NOW, YOU WILL ASSUME CONTROL OVER ALL OF DRYDEN'S TERRITORIES AND INTERESTS.
I APPRECIATE YOUR FAITH IN ME. I WON'T DISAPPOINT YOU.

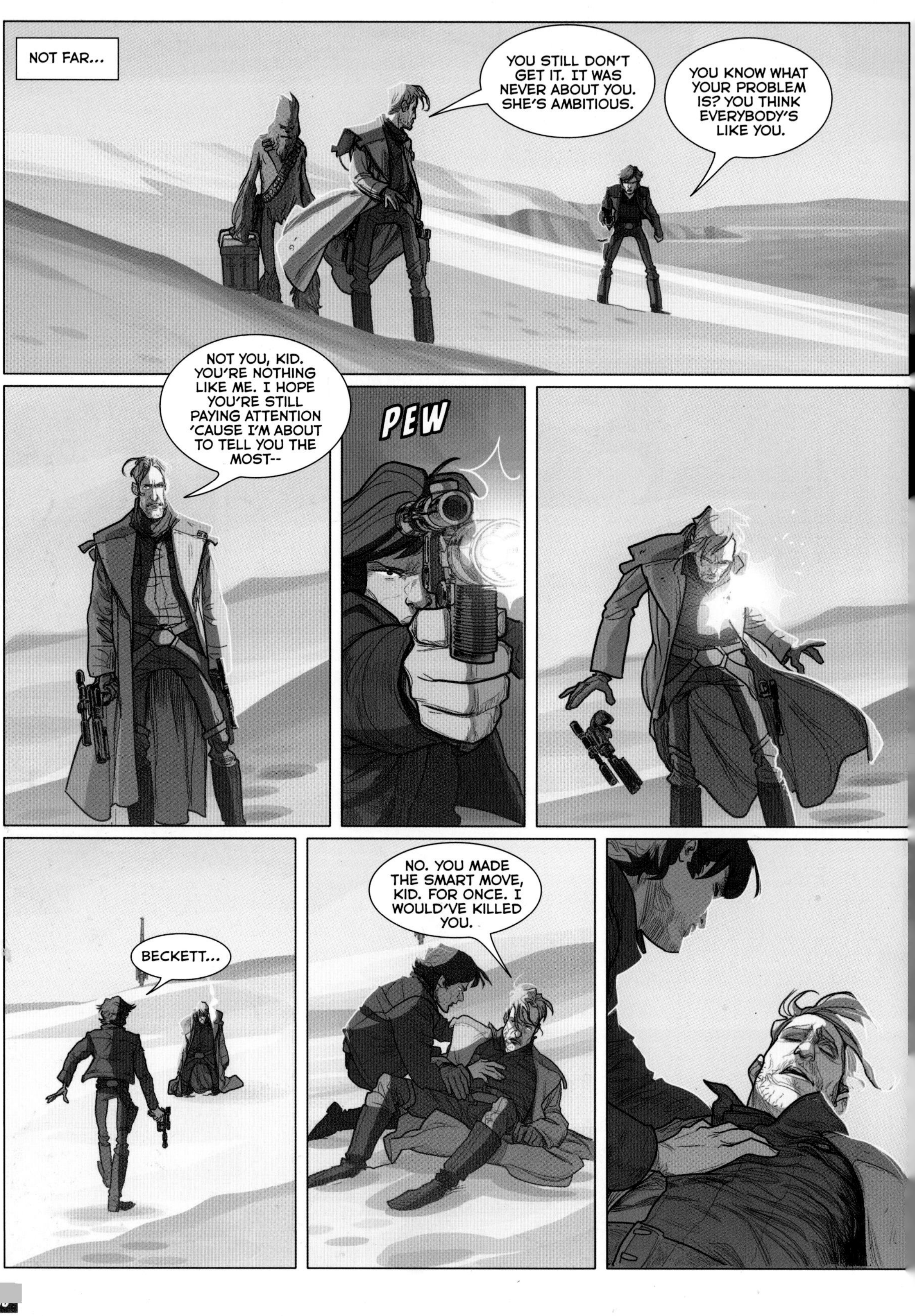

NOT FAR...
YOU STILL DON'T GET IT. IT WAS NEVER ABOUT YOU. SHE'S AMBITIOUS.
YOU KNOW WHAT YOUR PROBLEM IS? YOU THINK EVERYBODY'S LIKE YOU.
NOT YOU, KID. YOU'RE NOTHING LIKE ME. I HOPE YOU'RE STILL PAYING ATTENTION 'CAUSE I'M ABOUT TO TELL YOU THE MOST--
PEW
BECKETT...
NO. YOU MADE THE SMART MOVE, KID. FOR ONCE. I WOULD'VE KILLED YOU.

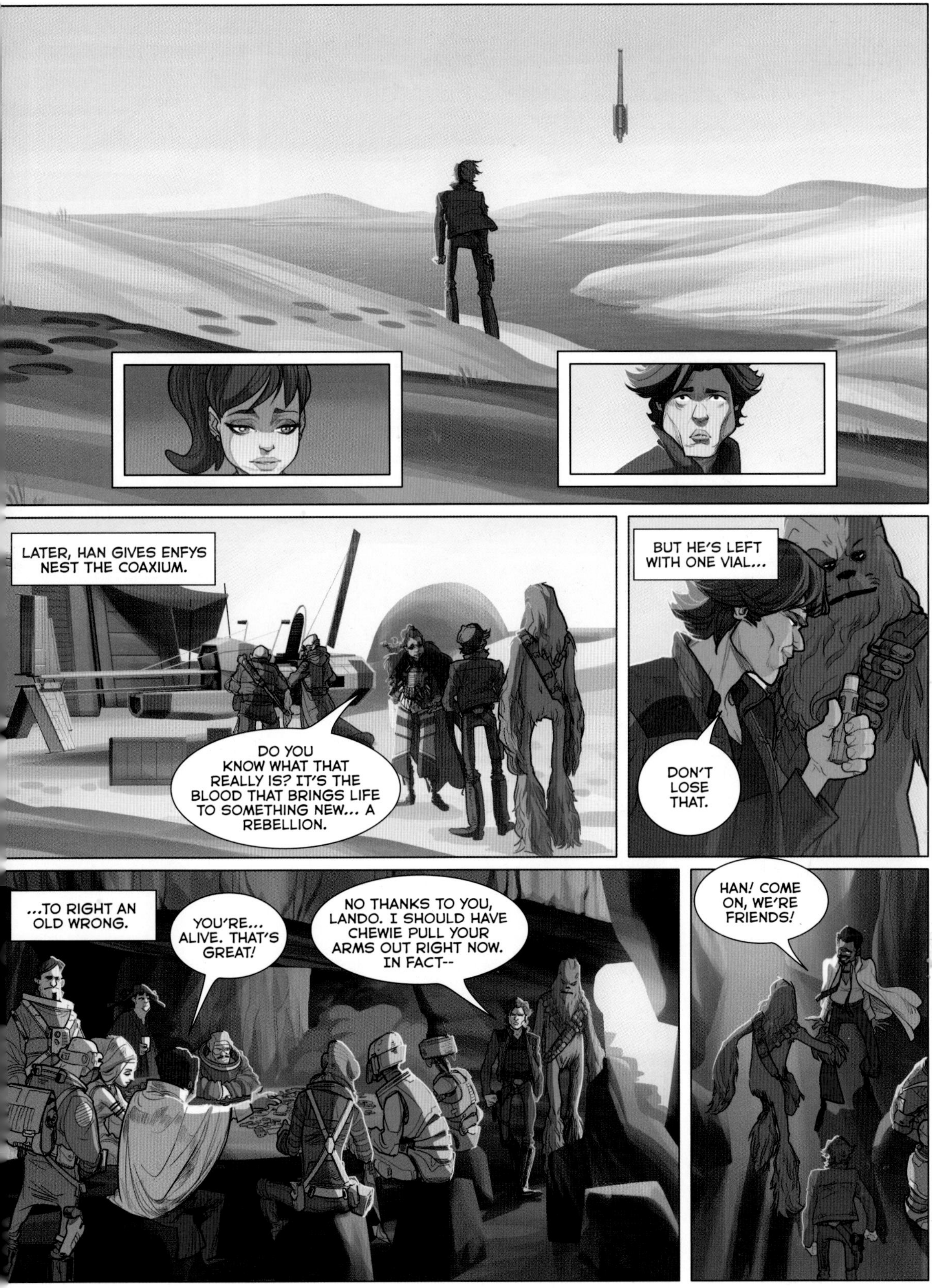
LATER, HAN GIVES ENFYS NEST THE COAXIUM.
DO YOU KNOW WHAT THAT REALLY IS? IT'S THE BLOOD THAT BRINGS LIFE TO SOMETHING NEW... A REBELLION.
BUT HE'S LEFT WITH ONE VIAL...
DON'T LOSE THAT.
...TO RIGHT AN OLD WRONG.
YOU'RE... ALIVE. THAT'S GREAT!
NO THANKS TO YOU, LANDO. I SHOULD HAVE CHEWIE PULL YOUR ARMS OUT RIGHT NOW. IN FACT--
HAN! COME ON, WE'RE FRIENDS!

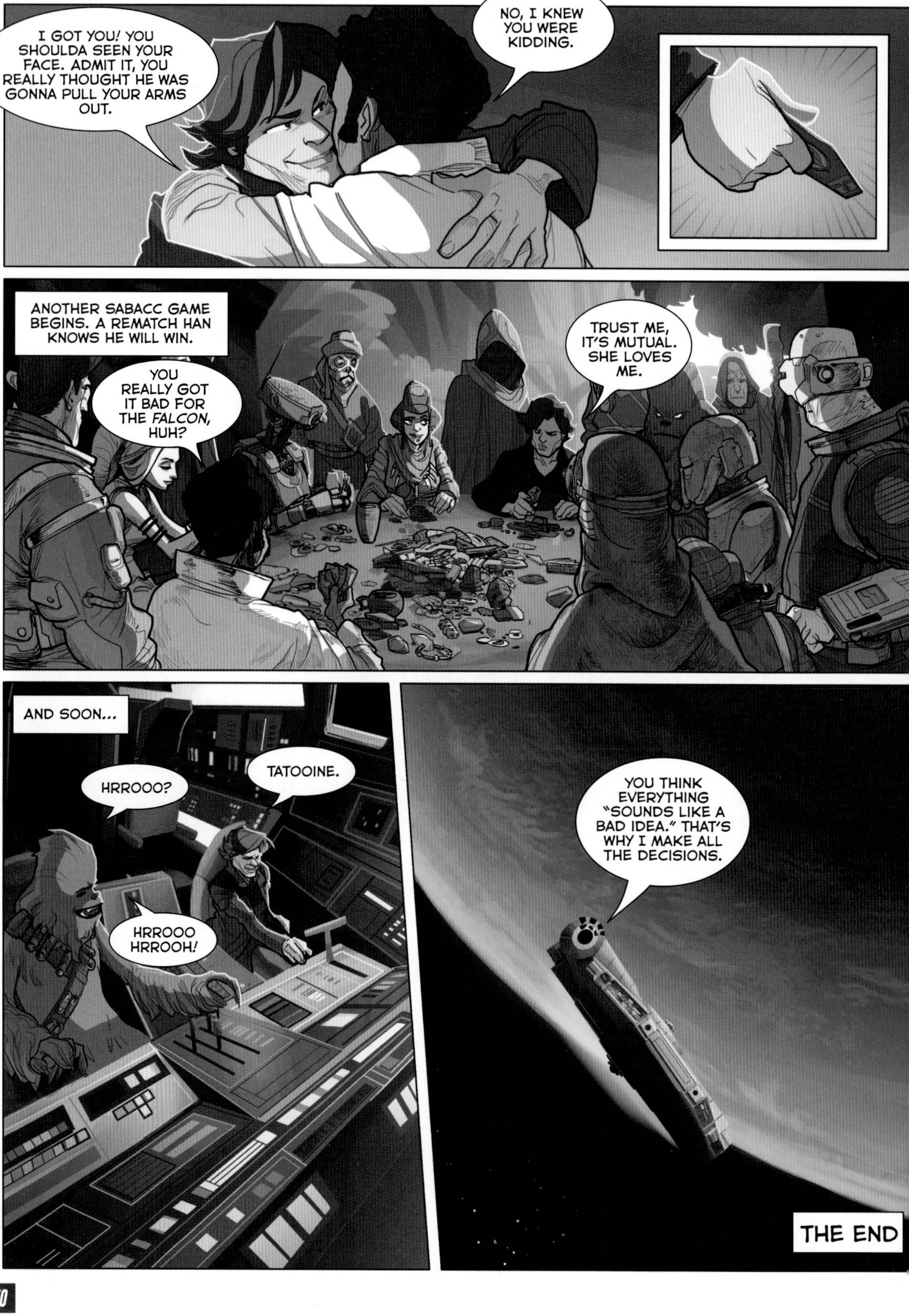
I GOT YOU! YOU SHOULDA SEEN YOUR FACE. ADMIT IT, YOU REALLY THOUGHT HE WAS GONNA PULL YOUR ARMS OUT.
NO, I KNEW YOU WERE KIDDING.
ANOTHER SABACC GAME BEGINS. A REMATCH HAN KNOWS HE WILL WIN.
YOU REALLY GOT IT BAD FOR THE *FALCON*, HUH?
TRUST ME, IT'S MUTUAL. SHE LOVES ME.
AND SOON...
HRROOO?
TATOOINE.
HRROOO HRROOH!
YOU THINK EVERYTHING "SOUNDS LIKE A BAD IDEA." THAT'S WHY I MAKE ALL THE DECISIONS.
THE END

"WE'LL JUST HAVE TO FIND A FASTER ROUTE."

HAN SOLO

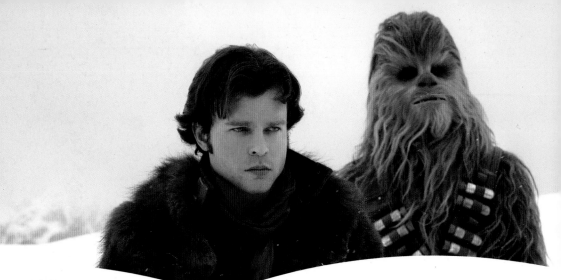

CREDITS

DISNEY PUBLISHING WORLDWIDE
Global Magazines, Comics and Partworks

Publisher
Lynn Waggoner
Editorial Director
Bianca Coletti
Editorial Team
Guido Frazzini (Director, Comics),
Stefano Ambrosio (Executive Editor, New IP),
Carlotta Quattrocolo (Executive Editor, Franchise),
Camilla Vedove (Senior Manager, Editorial Development),
Behnoosh Khalili (Senior Editor),
Julie Dorris (Senior Editor)
Design
Enrico Soave *(Senior Designer)*
Art
Ken Shue (VP, Global Art),
Roberto Santillo (Creative Director),
Marco Ghiglione (Creative Manager),
Manny Mederos (Creative Manager),
Stefano Attardi (Illustration Manager)
Portfolio Management
Olivia Ciancarelli *(Director)*
Business & Marketing
Mariantonietta Galla (Senior Manager, Franchise),
Virpi Korhonen (Editorial Manager)

Manuscript Adaptation
Alessandro Ferrari
Character Studies
Igor Chimisso
Layout
Matteo Piana
Clean Up and Ink
Igor Chimisso
Paint (background and settings)
Davide Turotti
Paint (characters)
Kawaii Creative Studio
Cover
Eric Jones
Special Thanks to
Michael Siglain, Jennifer Heddle,
James Waugh, Pablo Hidalgo,
Leland Chee, Matt Martin, Phil Szostak
For IDW:
Editors
Justin Eisinger and Alonzo Simon
Collection Design
Clyde Grapa
Publisher
Chris Ryall

Based on the screenplay by Jonathan Kasdan & Lawrence Kasdan

Based on characters created by George Lucas

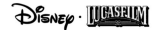

For international rights, contact **licensing@idwpublishing.com**

ISBN: 978-1-68405-391-9

22 21 20 19 1 2 3 4

Chris Ryall, President, Publisher & CCO • **John Barber**, Editor-in-Chief • **Robbie Robbins**, EVP/Sr. Graphic Artist • **Cara Morrison**, Chief Financial Officer **Matthew Ruzicka**, Chief Financial Officer • **Anita Frazier**, SVP of Sales and Marketing • **David Hedgecock**, Associate Publisher • **Jerry Bennington**, VP of New Product Development • **Lorelei Bunjes**, VP of Digital Services • **Justin Eisinger**, Editorial Director, Graphic Novels & Collections
Eric Moss, Senior Director, Licensing and Business Development

Ted Adams, IDW Founder

www.IDWPUBLISHING.com

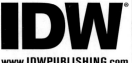

Facebook: facebook.com/idwpublishing • Twitter: @idwpublishing • YouTube: youtube.com/idwpublishing
Tumblr: tumblr.idwpublishing.com • Instagram: instagram.com/idwpublishing

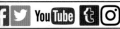